BY NANCY THAYER

A Nantucket Christmas
Island Girls
Summer Breeze
Heat Wave
Beachcombers
Summer House
Moon Shell Beach
The Hot Flash Club Chills Out
Hot Flash Holidays
The Hot Flash Club Strikes Again
The Hot Flash Club
Custody
Between Husbands and Friends
An Act of Love
Belonging
Family Secrets
Everlasting
My Dearest Friend
Spirit Lost
Morning
Nell
Bodies and Souls
Three Women at the Water's Edge
Stepping

A NANTUCKET CHRISTMAS

A Nantucket Christmas

A NOVEL

NANCY THAYER

BALLANTINE BOOKS
NEW YORK

A *Nantucket Christmas* is a work of fiction. Names, characters, places, and incidents are the products of the author's imagination or are used fictitiously. Any resemblance to actual events, locales, or persons, living or dead, is entirely coincidental.

Published in the United States by Ballantine Books, an imprint of The Random House Publishing Group, a division of Random House LLC, a Penguin Random House Company, New York.

BALLANTINE and the HOUSE colophon are registered trademarks of Random House LLC.

ISBN 978-0-345-54535-0
eBook ISBN 978-0-345-54546-6

Printed in the United States of America on acid-free paper

www.ballantinebooks.com

2 4 6 8 9 7 5 3 1

FIRST EDITION

Book design by Mary A. Wirth
Title-page art: © iStockphoto.com

For Meg Ruley

ACKNOWLEDGMENTS

Enormous thanks to my agent and fabulous friend Meg Ruley, who grew up on the island, for suggesting *A Nantucket Christmas*. She knows more than anyone how Nantucket can be a light in the darkness.

For years, my husband, Charley, and I gave a party on Christmas Eve. Our guests were, and are, the light in the darkness to me. Thanks to Charlotte Maison, who over the years became Charlotte Kastner, and her husband, Tom Kastner. Thanks to her son Karl Schoonover and his partner Lloyd Pratt. Thank you to Pam Pindell and her daughters Rebecca Sayre and Casey Sayre, and Casey's husband, Steve Boukus, and their children Torin and Kyra. Thanks to M.J. and Del Wynn and their sons Patrick and Riley. Thanks to Laura Simon, Jim Gross, and Susan Simon. Thanks to Suze Robinson and Kat Robinson Grieder and James Grieder and their son, Will. Thanks to Dionis Gauvin, who I hope will bring her husband, Mike Mills, one year. Thanks to our son, Josh Thayer, and his partner David Gillum. Thanks to Jonathan, Katie, and Elizabeth Hemingway, and to Jonathan's mother, Nancy Rappaport. Thanks to Leslie Linsley, Jon Aron, and Gretchen Anderson. Thanks to Mimi and Dwight Beman and their daughters Allie, Elizabeth, and Ann, and Ann's husband, Roger Nina and their daughter, Natalia. Thanks to our daughter Sam and her husband, Neil Forbes, and their children Ellias, Adeline, and Emmett, who have begun, understandably, having Christmas Eve parties at their house on the mainland.

Everything changes. New people come and beloved people go far too soon. The island stays—and a pun is in that word.

I also want to thank my publishing family at Ballantine who has provided so much wisdom, laughter, and support: my radiant editor Linda Marrow, Gina Centrello, Libby McGuire, and Dana Isaacson. Thanks to Junessa Viloria, Kim Hovey, Penelope Haynes, Alison Masciovecchio, Ashley Woodfolk, and Quinne Rogers.

Much gratitude goes to the Jane Rotrosen Agency, especially my agent, Meg Ruley, and to Christian Hogrebe and Peggy Gordijn.

Thank you, Wendy Schmidt and Wendy Hudson, for keeping independent bookstores alive on Nantucket.

Thank you, Charley, for everything.

And Merry Christmas to everyone, from Nantucket.

A NANTUCKET CHRISTMAS

PROLOGUE

❄

This tale begins, as do many Nantucket tails, with a dog. A Norwich terrier, the runt of the litter—which made him very small indeed—a stubby, sturdy, tan, pint-sized pup with a face like a fox's, ears like a panda's, and the dark passionate eyes of Antonio Banderas.

His name was Snix.

Back in his chubby days, he was adopted by the Collins family visiting from Rhode Island. His plump bumbling made Cota, their teenage daughter, squeal that he was *so cute*. Cota named him Snix because she knew no other dog in the world had ever been named Snix. Cota was at the age when she wanted to be noticed for being the kind of special girl who would have a dog named Snix.

At the beginning of the family's summer vacation, Cota doted on Snix, letting him sleep in her bed, brushing his coarse coat, tickling his fat belly, and taking him for lots of walks up and down Main Street on Nantucket, with Snix tripping fetchingly over his rhinestone leash.

Three months later, Cota was fourteen instead of thirteen. Her hair was two inches longer, her legs were three inches longer, her bosom was three inches fuller, and she didn't need a pet of any kind to get noticed. Meanwhile, Snix had lost his puppy fat and his roly-poly ways. He now wore a mournful and slightly baffled expression, having gone from adored to ignored in three short months.

At the end of the summer, the Collins family did what many vacationers do when they return home from their holiday—they left their adopted pet behind. They drove their black SUV out to the moors in the middle of the island, where dirt roads ranged over low hills and past small ponds, where rabbits, moles, and deer hid in the bushes. They removed Snix's collar, name tag, and leash before Cota opened the door, leaned out, and set the pup on the dry, end-of-summer grass.

"Bye, Snix," the teenager chirped hastily, slamming the door shut.

The family's large black SUV roared off, leaving a cloud of sandy dust floating in the air.

Snix sat with his head cocked, watching. Waiting. Expectant. Then, not so expectant, more hopeful. Then, sad. Snix lay down with his head on his paws, his eyes fixed steadily on the dirt road where his family's car had last been—he could still smell the gas fumes, and Cota's light fragrance.

No other cars passed. It was just after Labor Day. Everyone had left the island. Well, not everyone, of course—twelve thousand people still lived and worked on the island, but none were strolling that hot day on a secluded sandy track through the moors.

September was much like August on the island of Nantucket. The sun beat down on the crackling brown grass and on Snix. Overhead, small planes zipped back and forth, taking people from the island back to the mainland. From time to time a sparrow would tweet and flutter from one tree to another. Snix watched a spider creep across the dirt road and disappear in the bayberry bushes. That was about it for action that afternoon.

Snix was by no means a stupid dog, but he was naturally loyal and he was young and naive. He didn't have the experience even to consider the possibility that the sweet-smelling long-haired girl who hugged him and cuddled him and chucked him under his chinny-chin-chin was never coming back for him.

So he waited. His stomach growled. He got very thirsty. He smelled water, fresh water, nearby, but he didn't want to leave this spot in case the Collins family came back for him. So he lay there, a little brown puppy more gangling than chubby, more dog than baby, more awkward than adorable. He lay there with his head on his paws until the sun set and the world around him turned black and he saw no lights anywhere. He'd never been in a world without lights, and that made him shiver, and that made him whimper, and then he let out such a disconsolate howl that he frightened himself and a few other critters nearby.

He began running very fast down the road, toward the scent of human civilization.

1

❄

On Nantucket, the Christmas season is different.

Really.

The island, fifty-two square miles of flat sandy land, lies in windswept isolation almost thirty miles away from the continent and all its institutions and entertainments. In the summer, the sun shines down on golden beaches and a serene blue sea. In the winter, gale force winds lash and howl over the ocean, cutting its residents off from family, friends, and often fresh bread and milk as Nantucket Sound freezes over and no planes fly, no boats sail, to or from the island. When the sun sets early and rises late, deep black water surrounds the land in infinite darkness.

Then Nantucket comes truly alive. Islanders have the leisure to savor the Charles Dickens charm gleaming from the glistening cobblestone streets and historic brick buildings. They relish the coziness of the small town where they know everyone, and everyone's dog. After a hectic summer, they enjoy the tranquil pace. They take time to stop, look, listen, pat the dog, tickle a baby's chin, chat, and laugh. They attend Christmas pageants, holiday fairs, and all manner of cabarets. The town lines the central streets of the village with dozens of small evergreens twinkling with multicolored lights and weatherproof decorations. The islanders pause to gaze up at the forty-foot spruce blazing at the top of Main Street, and they nod in appreciation and gratitude.

They celebrate light, life, and laughter as the winter dark wildness descends.

The Christmas Stroll began as an occasion for merchants to welcome islanders into their shops for hot buttered rum, spiced apple cider, warm gossip, and good cheer. Store windows were artistically decorated with mermaids and Santas, seahorses and fairy-tale scenes. Mr. and Mrs. Santa arrived on a Coast Guard boat and were delivered to the Jared Coffin House by horse and buggy. The aroma of fresh fish chowder and island-brewed beer wafted enticingly from the restaurants. The town crier strode through the streets in tall hat and cape, and Victorian carolers enchanted the salt air with song.

Not surprisingly, and oddly around the same time the one-hour fast ferries started their rounds, news of Nantucket's Christmas Stroll spread to off-island friends and relatives of the townspeople. One sparkling winter day, a Boston television station sent a reporter and cameraman. After that, the annual event was famous.

For children, it was magic. For adults, it was a chance to be childlike.

For Nicole Somerset, the Nantucket Christmas Stroll was close to miraculous.

❄

Four years ago, Nicole was a widow. Her friend Jilly insisted that Nicole travel down from Boston for the weekend to enjoy the Stroll. Nicole came, and fell in love with the charming small town, its festively bedecked windows, its fresh salt air and chiming church bells. She fell in love with a man, as well.

She met Sebastian Somerset at a party. They liked each other a lot, rather quickly, if not immediately, but being older, and possibly wiser, they took time getting to know each other. Nicole was widowed and childless. Sebastian was divorced, with a grown daughter.

Nicole was a nurse. She had just retired at fifty-five, but she missed her patients and colleagues. She missed her work, too. She liked to keep busy. Sebastian, sixty-two, had worked for a Boston law firm. He had also just retired, realizing he'd spent too much of his life working. He wanted to enjoy life.

Slowly, cautiously, they began to date, discovering that *together* they enjoyed life a great deal. Sebastian owned a house on the island, and as the days, weeks, and then months went by, he introduced Nicole to the pleasures the island offered—swimming, sailing, and tennis. In turn, Nicole introduced Sebastian to the delights his first wife had disdained: homemade pie, eaten while watching large-screen television; walking rather than biking through the island moors; stopping to notice the birds and wildflowers rather than jogging to keep his heart rate up; or watching the sun set on the beach rather than attending a cocktail party.

Sebastian's first wife, Katya, was a perfectionist who had kept him on a tight leash and a rigid routine. After a few months of relaxed satisfaction with Nicole, Sebastian worried he would gain weight and develop heart trouble. To his surprise, he gained no weight, and his blood pressure actually dropped. When he asked his doctor about this at his annual check-up, Maury Molson leaned back in his chair and shrewdly raised his hairy eyebrows.

"Sebastian, you've been going through life as if everything is a competition. During this past year, you've stopped to smell the roses, and it's been the best thing you could do for your health."

Sebastian chortled in surprise. "I'm shocked."

"Me, too," Maury told him. "I don't believe I've ever

heard you laugh like that before. And it's true, happiness is the best medicine."

When Sebastian told Nicole about this, she beamed and responded, "You make me happy, too. Although I haven't had my blood pressure checked."

"I wish we could live together for the rest of our lives," Sebastian allowed, looking worried.

"Darling, why can't we?"

Sebastian had furrowed his brow. "I think you should meet my daughter before we go any further."

Sebastian and Katya had a daughter, Kennedy, who was, Sebastian uneasily confessed, emotionally complicated. A carbon copy of her blond, beautiful mother, Kennedy tried to emulate Katya, meaning that she tried to be perfect, still not understanding, after all the years of living with her, that it was so much easier for a woman to be perfect when she focused only on herself.

Because Katya had been a kind but cool mother, Sebastian had, he admitted, cossetted, pampered, and perhaps even spoiled Kennedy a bit. Okay, perhaps a lot. Now married to a perpetually flustered stockbroker named James, Kennedy found herself overwhelmed herself by the responsibilities of grocery shopping, cooking, cleaning, and caring for their son Maddox.

Kennedy was further dismayed by her parents' divorce.

Katya had been thoughtful enough to wait until Kennedy's wedding five years ago to leave Sebastian for her tennis coach, Alonzo. Kennedy couldn't understand why her father, who could always do anything and everything, couldn't win Katya back. When Sebastian had admitted to Kennedy that he didn't *want* Katya back, that he was more contented without her, Kennedy had dissolved into a weeping fit and said she never wanted to see her father again.

Kennedy changed her mind when her baby boy was born. She didn't want her son to grow up without his grandparents, even if they were no longer married. For the past four years, Sebastian's relationship with his daughter had been close and comfortable. Kennedy had even accepted Alonzo's presence in her mother's life, although she told her father it broke her heart every time she saw Katya with that other man.

So naturally, Sebastian worried about telling Kennedy about Nicole.

Sebastian paced the living room of Nicole's Boston apartment as he strategized the first meeting. "I've told Kennedy I've been seeing someone. I'm going to tell her I want to bring you to dinner, to meet her. That should indicate that I'm serious about you."

Nicole had no advice to give. She had not been able to have children. All her nurturing instincts had gone into her nursing profession. She thought Kennedy sounded like a difficult personality, but how bad could she be?

"Tell Kennedy I'd like to bring dessert," Nicole offered.

"Why would you do that?" Sebastian looked genuinely puzzled.

"It's a nice thing to do," Nicole explained gently. She'd begun to see that in Sebastian's former social-climbing world, *niceness* had no place. His life with Katya had been all about ambition. "It will save her from cooking something."

Sebastian thought this over. "I see."

When she stepped into Kennedy's home, it was Nicole who *saw,* and her heart plummeted for the man she'd come to love and for his daughter. Clearly Kennedy had copied her mother's style of décor, best described as "Glacial Chic." Walls, furniture, floors, even wall *art,* were white. The living room coffee table was glass with sharp edges. The dining room chairs and tablecloth were black; the plates white. It was a hot summer evening when she first entered Kennedy's home, and Nicole wished she'd brought a pashmina to ward off the chill.

Kennedy, blond and wire-hanger thin, wore a white sleeveless dress. Her husband, James, wore a starched white button-down shirt with khakis. Only little Maddox, chubby in his navy blue and white sailor outfit, provided a dash of color.

Everyone shook hands politely, and then Nicole sank to her knees in front of Maddox.

"Hi, Maddox. I've brought you a present." She held out a brightly colored gift bag. She'd spent hours considering what to bring for the child, knowing as she did all the restrictions his mother placed on his life. Maddox was two then, much too young, Kennedy insisted, to watch any television. Also, he could not have any candy or anything sweet. Also, he was not to have anything "technological"—no remote-controlled cars or dump trucks, no handheld video games.

Wanting to get him something special, Nicole had bought him a silly-faced, shaggy-haired white goat which, when a button was pushed, burst into "High on a hill was a lonely goatherd" and continued singing through the entire song, wagging its head and batting its long black eyelashes.

Maddox clapped his hands and giggled when he saw it. Kennedy opened her mouth to object, but after a moment could think of no objection, and managed to say, "Tell Nicole thank you, Maddox."

"Thank you," Maddox said.

Nicole beamed as she rose to her feet. She had passed the first test. Proudly, she wrapped her arm through Sebastian's arm, giving it a quick smug hug.

"Love-dovey—ick!" Maddox giggled.

Nicole started to pull her arm away.

But Sebastian laughed and with his other arm reached out and pulled his daughter next to him. "Maddox, I like hugs from my women."

Nicole watched emotions flicker over Kennedy's lovely face: surprise at her father's unusual spontaneity; joy at being hugged by her father; consternation at being hugged when her father was with Nicole.

Dinner was a complicated casserole with a French name and a salad of puzzling gourmet lettuce called frisée that felt like sharp bitter hair in Nicole's mouth. Still, she appreciated the trouble Kennedy had gone to.

"This meat is so tender," Nicole complimented Kennedy.

Kennedy actually blushed. "Thank you. It's *daub au poivre*. The meat is marinated with wine and all sorts of herbs. I had to find lard for the recipe. *Lard*. Who uses lard anymore? But I wanted to make it authentic . . ."

She's nervous, Nicole realized, as Kennedy babbled on. Not nervous about Nicole, but about the excellence of her cooking. Kennedy's eyes flitted to her father as she spoke, waiting for him to praise her. Nicole kicked Sebastian in the ankle until he spoke up.

"It's delicious, Kennedy. Never tasted anything better."

Nicole could see Kennedy's shoulders actually relax, dropping a few inches away from her ears. A tender spot blossomed in her heart for the young woman.

But when time came for dessert, Kennedy refused to taste Nicole's deep-dish apple pie.

Putting her hand on her waistline, Kennedy said, "I don't eat desserts. We all know that sugar is bad for us. And I have to watch my weight, like mother does. I don't want to get"—she glanced at Nicole's rounder figure—"pudgy."

Sebastian chuckled around a mouth of delicious pie. "We all gain weight as we grow older, darling."

"Mother hasn't," Kennedy reminded him. "She's got a gorgeous shape and a flat tummy."

She probably doesn't eat *lard*, Nicole wanted to say, but kept her mouth shut.

And that, as far as Nicole was concerned, summed up her relationship with Kennedy. One step forward, one step back.

❄

Nicole and Sebastian married. The January ceremony was attended by only a few intimate friends since they assumed Kennedy would refuse to attend. Katya was blissfully redecorating her Boston townhouse and continuing to see Alonzo. Kennedy's husband, James, was doing well with his work, and Maddox was growing out of the toddler stage, becoming more manageable. A delicate harmony existed in Sebastian's inner circle; Nicole and Sebastian did not want to disrupt the peace.

Nicole sold her small apartment and moved to Sebastian's Nantucket house to live year-round. She made friends, loved the small town, and began to anticipate the holiday season.

This year Katya and Alonzo were going to a tennis and cleansing spa. That meant that Kennedy, James, and Maddox were coming to the island for Christmas week.

The entire seven-day-long Christmas *week*.

2

❄

Why did his parents need another baby? Maddox wondered about this constantly. It was going to be a boy, too, his mommy had told him. Wasn't Maddox a good enough boy for his parents?

He tried to be a good boy. He ate his vegetables, even though they sometimes made him gag. He strained desperately to comprehend the funny squiggles on the page every day when his mommy tried to teach him to read, and he had already mastered the art of using the potty. Most of the time.

But Maddox had seen babies. They couldn't use the potty at all. So why did his parents want one?

"You'll have someone to play with," his mommy promised. But a kid couldn't play with a *baby*. Babies couldn't throw a ball. They couldn't even lift their heads.

It was a puzzle.

He'd suggested many times that instead the family

could get a dog. With all his heart, Maddox wanted a dog. He could throw a stick for a dog and play ball with a dog and cuddle in bed with a dog . . . although maybe not. Mommy said they would bring dirt and germs into the house.

Nicole had given Maddox had a stuffed goat and even though Mommy said Nicole was a hag, he loved the animal, which sang—until Mommy removed the battery. Maddox named him Yodel and held him when he went to bed at night, rubbing Yodel's silky tongue between his thumb and finger. It helped him fall asleep.

He knew, of course, that a real goat wouldn't have a satin tongue, and he wouldn't be able to rub the tongue, anyway, that would get drool all over the bed. Anyway, he didn't want a real goat, which was too big. He wanted a small dog, so he could put his arm around it and feel its furry warmth against his body. He would like that.

When he was little, his mommy had held him in her arms a lot. Now that she was all stuffed with the baby, holding Maddox was too hard for her. She didn't have a lap to sit on anymore, and Maddox was always, she said, poking him with his elbows or knees. He tried to be careful, but now Mommy said she was getting breathless since the baby's bum was pushing against her lungs.

"I love you, Maddox, but you're *too much* for Mommy." That's what she said yesterday. He was *too much* when he made a *zoom zoom* noise with his cars. He was *too much* when he wouldn't eat asparagus.

Ugh, asparagus was so gaggy, like a long package of strings that caught in his throat. Maddox shuddered, remembering.

He hoped when they went to Granddad and Nicole's house for Christmas he would get to eat other stuff. Maybe cake or pie. Nicole was nice to Maddox, even if she wasn't a real grandmother. She had sent Maddox his very own Christmas card, and it had a cute puppy on it, sticking out of a Christmas stocking.

"That woman is just trying to make trouble," Maddox's mommy said with a frown when she saw Nicole's card. Maddox didn't understand how a card could cause trouble. He hid it under his mattress so his mommy wouldn't throw it away.

3

❄

As they drove home from the firm's Christmas party, Kennedy didn't speak but allowed her frustration to steam out of her body as if she were an overheated pressure cooker, which she was.

"Kennedy," her husband James pleaded. "Talk to me. Did you honestly have such a bad time?"

"I had a *terrible* time. I'm fat, my face is covered with blotches, I can't breathe, and all the secretaries oozed around you with their four-inch heels and cute skimpy dresses, smirking and flaunting their cleavage."

James sighed loudly. "Kennedy, hon. You're almost eight months pregnant. Your hormones are making you crazy. No one flirted with me. Plus, I saw several secretaries and quite a few lawyers stop by to talk to you."

James was right, but that didn't make Kennedy feel any better. "I feel so ugly," she wailed.

"You know you're beautiful," James assured her in a bored tone. He'd been having to say this a lot recently.

Kennedy closed her eyes and let her head fall back against the seat. Why couldn't she be like her mother, who was always perfect?

The last time they had visited her mother, Katya had taken out her photograph albums to show Kennedy what she had looked like during her pregnancy, and of course Katya was glorious and glowing, seeming energetic and fit enough for another set of tennis.

Kennedy looked like Shrek.

Her obstetrician assured Kennedy the expected baby boy was of normal size, but she felt as if she were carrying a full-grown linebacker rigged with shoulderpads and helmet.

"You'll feel better when we're on Nantucket," James said soothingly. "Your father and Nicole will pamper you."

"But I don't like that woman," Kennedy protested.

"You scarcely know Nicole," James reminded her.

Kennedy whimpered. "I want my parents to be together."

James exhaled, losing patience. "That's not going to happen. We've been over this before."

Fine. Then Kennedy wanted to be with her mother. But Katya was much too busy playing tennis with her *lover*, Alonzo, and furnishing her new Boston condo. The fact that her mother didn't want Kennedy around made Kennedy hate her father's new wife even more. She knew, somehow, this wasn't logical, but who ever said emotions were logical, especially during pregnancy?

Kennedy glanced over at her husband, seeing his strong profile as the streetlights flashed past. She could tell by the way his jaw was clenched that he was exasperated with her. She couldn't blame him. She might be a pain in his neck, but *she* had pain everywhere! He wanted this second child as much as she did, but she had to do all the heavy lifting. Literally.

James didn't understand the stress of parenting. Choosing the right preschool; keeping her child away from the evils of sugar, fat, and pesticide-spiked protein. Trying to keep the world safe by not buying plastic, while at the same time trying to give her child fun toys to play with. Keeping her four-year-old away from the damages television could inflict on an innocent mind, protecting her son from the sight of monsters, swords, and cannons . . . The list was endless. It was all up to her, because James was so busy supporting the family.

And now it was the Christmas season! Maddox was begging for a puppy, but Kennedy was going to have a baby. How could she cope with puppy poop as well as a new baby?

Sometimes she just wanted to cry and cry.

"Buck up, Kennedy." James clicked the remote that opened their garage door and guided his BMW into its berth. "We're home. You can go to bed."

Right. There was another issue: bed. Bed with James. They hadn't made love in forever. Why *wouldn't* James want to have an affair with one of those sleek young secretaries in those tight-fitting dresses?

Kennedy burst into tears.

4

❄

NICOLE'S TO-DO LIST

Make ten dozen cookies for Stroll.
Make Buche du Noel and freeze.
Make beef Wellington and freeze.
Lose ten pounds.
Make gingerbread house; use sugarless candy for decorations.
Find sugarless candy.
Christmas tree.
Laurel around stair banister?
Find freezable breakfast casserole recipes.
Start buttock-tightening exercises.

Early on the morning of the Nantucket Christmas Stroll, glittering crystal sunlight streamed through the mist onto the shops, streets, houses, and harbor, a mirror-like light it seemed you could almost touch with your fingertips.

But then the temperature plummeted and white clouds pillowed the sky, shaking out feather-like snowflakes.

Standing in her Nantucket kitchen, Nicole snapped the Saran Wrap off the roll with such force the sheet flew up in her face.

Live in the now, she admonished herself. *Cherish the day*.

Smell the damned roses.

She unpeeled the plastic from her nose and carefully covered the last platter of cookies for the library bake sale at the Stroll. She poured herself another cup of coffee, sank into a kitchen chair, and forced herself to appreciate her surroundings.

Honey-warm wide-board floors laid in 1840, a fireplace with a simple Greek Revival mantel, and an antique pine table mingled perfectly with state-of-the-art appliances and slate countertops. It was Nicole's good fortune that Katya chose to keep the Boston house in the divorce and Sebastian decided to live here permanently. The house was a masterpiece—especially, Nicole mused with a satisfied grin, the brand-new bed she'd insisted on having installed in the master bedroom.

Nicole had made other changes in the décor. Though small and inexpensive, they had transformed the house from a museum-like sterility into a welcoming home. She placed plump cushions in jaunty patchwork designs on the chairs around the kitchen table, filled colorful pottery jars with flour, sugar, and other staples to brighten the counter, and hung an oil painting of an oystercatcher by Bobby Frazier on the wall. The comical seabird, with its orange legs and beak, amused anyone who saw it.

Nicole had lightened the rest of the house with similar changes: She'd removed most of the useless antiques sitting around collecting dust—how many brass lanterns, cobbler's lasts, and hard-bottomed old benches did any one house need? She'd added a couple of deeply comfortable chintz-covered armchairs to replace the wooden ladder-back cane-bottomed relics in the living room, plush pillows softened the white sofas, and Claire Murray rugs woven with coastal scenes, Nantucket hydrangeas, or mermaids brought seaside color to the rooms.

Yes, she'd made the house hers. Hers and Sebastian's. And with that thought, her mood flipped into happiness. She picked up the phone and speed-dialed her best friend on the island.

"Jilly," Nicole said, "I've finished the cookies for the Stroll."

"Fab," Jilly said. "Want me to drive over and help you get them to the Atheneum?"

"No, thanks," Nicole said. "Seb can help me tomorrow morning. I'm just calling to vent."

"Vent away," Jilly urged.

"I've got so much to do and I don't think I can accomplish it all," Nicole worried. "Katya was such a Martha Stewart purist. I'm a clodhopper by comparison."

"You're a nurse," Jilly reminded her. "You can save lives. Plus, you've made Sebastian truly happy."

Jilly spoke with authority. She'd known Sebastian when he was married to Katya. She considered Katya lovely but profoundly socially inept. Katya strived to be the best at everything, but her frosty empress façade hid an even frostier heart. Men lusted after her and woman were intimidated by her, but anyone who spent over five minutes with her went away feeling shorter, fatter, and flawed.

"Kennedy phoned Seb last night," Nicole confided. "She says she wants both her mother and her father to be with her during the birth of her second baby."

"When's the due date?"

"January tenth. I know Kennedy hopes her parents will get back together, and what better bonding moment than the birth of their second grandchild?"

"I get the picture. A major family event and you're left out."

"Exactly."

"What can you do?" asked Jilly.

"In reality? Nothing." Nicole looked toward the kitchen window. If today's crisp weather lasted through tomorrow, it would be ideal for the Stroll. "So I should stop obsessing over that and go back to obsessing over Christmas."

"What are you getting Maddox for Christmas?"

"Kennedy insists we buy only wooden toys."

"Oh, please. What does Seb say?"

"Um, let's see: variations on 'don't worry about it' and 'it will be fine.' "

"Perhaps he's right," Jilly said. "After all, this is the season of miracles."

❄

Seb drove Nicole to the library before it opened. He parked on India Street and helped her carry in her platters of cookies decorated like wreaths, trees, snowmen and snowwomen. This allowed him the opportunity to dash down to the used book sale in the basement of the Atheneum a few moments before the crowds arrived.

Nicole stood on the front porch of the library behind a table laden with her cookies, chatting with Jilly, who was manning the hot chocolate urn. Nicole wore her red wool trapeze coat and a red Santa cap with white fake fur trim. Jilly wore a green wool coat, a headband shaped like reindeer antlers, and earrings, one red, one green, fashioned like Christmas tree lights. They flashed off and on.

This was conservative attire for the Stroll, when townspeople and tourists alike descended on Main Street to celebrate the season. Nicole and Jilly served hot chocolate and cookies to elves, polar bears, the puppeteer Joe Vito and his gigantic puppet Grunge, and to the carolers costumed in Victorian garb, with long velvet cloaks, bonnets, and top hats. Posh off-islanders wore fur coats and diamond pins shaped like snowflakes. Even the more staid citizens sported red mittens, green and white striped mufflers, and red wool caps.

At eleven, Seb appeared on the library porch. "Ready?"

"Absolutely. Here comes my replacement." Nicole hugged her friend, took Seb's hand, and they went down the wooden library steps and through the picket fence to the brick sidewalk.

"Which way?" Seb asked.

Nicole linked her hand through her husband's arm. "Let's go see Santa arrive."

They sauntered along, taking it all in, waving at friends. Several of the streets were blocked off for the gathering crowds whose pleasure was reflected back to them by the shining shop windows. Clever wreaths of evergreen or seashells or buoys decorated the doors, and dozens of small Christmas trees twinkled up and down the six major streets of the town. A fiddler strolled through the town playing folk tunes. The town crier strode around in his long black cape, waiting to ring the bell to announce the arrival of Santa.

"Look, Sebastian!" Nicole pointed at a Great Dane in a Santa Claus hat and a cherry-red Rudolph nose.

"Nantucketers love their dogs," Sebastian told her.

Nicole spotted dogs decked out with reindeer ears and red velvet bows, hand-knit sweaters and blinking lights. A corgi wore a jingle bell collar that tinkled as she waddled along. "The dogs seem quite pleased to be in costume," Nicole observed.

The town sheriff, Jim Perelman, waved at Sebastian and Nicole. "The boat's on its way!" he called to them.

Nicole tugged Sebastian's hand. "Hurry."

Straight Wharf was already crowded with families. Daddies held children on their shoulders, older kids worked hard to appear blasé, dogs sniffed the ground in search of dropped cookie crumbs. Everyone looked to the harbor waters, watching for the Coast Guard boat that brought Santa and Mrs. Claus.

"Here it comes," Sebastian told Nicole. He waved. "There's John West, he's the captain."

"The one with the candy-cane-striped muffler?" Nicole asked.

"Right."

The vessel motored steadily through the waves toward the pier, the Coast Guard decked out in red jackets and Santa Claus hats. The American flag with its red and white stripes rippled gaily in the breeze.

The boat docked. The ramp was secured. The crowd applauded as Santa and his wife stepped off the boat and were escorted into a carriage pulled by a handsome black horse. They processed up the cobblestone street toward the historic Jared Coffin House, where Santa would sit children on his knee and listen to their Christmas wishes.

"This certainly puts me in a holiday mood." Nicole squeezed her husband's hand from sheer delight. "Let's stop and listen to the bell ringers."

They paused at the top of Main Street, where a glittering Christmas tree towered in front of the Pacific Bank. The peals of the bells floated like golden bubbles through the frosty air.

"Lunch, I think," Sebastian said, tugging Nicole away from the music.

At 12 Degrees East, they dined on creamy clam chowder and healthy green salads, sipped glasses of sparkling Prosecco, and treated themselves to bread pudding topped with whipped cream.

"I feel a nap coming on," Sebastian confessed.

"I feel the need to shop!" Nicole countered.

"Nicole." Sebastian shook his head fondly. "You mustn't get carried away with this Christmas business."

Nicole swirled milk and sugar into her coffee. "Tell me about your Christmases with Katya."

Sebastian shrugged. "No big deal. When Kennedy was small, we went to either my parents' or Katya's for the holidays. After our parents died and Kennedy was older and more manageable, we took family trips over Christmas. To Fiji, and Paris, and Aruba, that sort of thing."

"Did Katya decorate the house?" Nicole restrained any tone of judgment from her voice.

Sebastian considered her question. "Somewhat. Candles, that sort of thing. She never put up a tree because the needles would fall off, making a mess on the carpet. And after all, the trips were the main event."

Nicole put her hand over Sebastian's. "You know, Gordie and I never had any children. I always loved the Christmas season, but I missed being able to share it with a child. Now that Maddox is coming, I'm eager to get a big tree and do it up right, and buy lots of presents for him. And for the new baby. Maybe something fabulous and sparkly for Kennedy, too, to buoy her up since she's so weighed down with her pregnancy."

As she spoke, Nicole's face brightened. She loved giving gifts.

Sebastian's face lit up, too. "Sweetheart, you're such a dreamer. Sure, let's get a great big evergreen and you can trim the tree to your heart's content." He leaned forward. "What would *you* like for Christmas?"

Less than a year old, their marriage was still new. Nicole blushed. "I have everything I want," she told her husband.

5

❄

On that dreadful September day, Snix had run like a wild thing so fast and so far he'd finally come to the end of the moors. Here on the hilltops, huge mansions overlooked the world around them. Many were in the process of being shut up for the winter and refrigerators were cleaned out, their contents tossed into garbage containers that were easily opened. For a few weeks, Snix sniffed out sufficient food to sustain him.

Wandering this way, he found himself approaching the main cluster of population, where houses gathered closely together along winding lanes. As the days went by and the leaves turned colors and drifted down, some of these houses emptied out also. Still, many houses were lived in. Snix could tell by the smells. Some dogs even possessed homes, great massive structures with yards where entry was forbidden by their urinary territorial postings. He avoided those places.

He could usually find a comfortable wicker chair on a back porch to sleep in for the night. He searched the center of the town for food, hitting the jackpot where the ferries and boats docked. There, the trash barrels were always full.

The trees grew bare. The temperature fell. The lights disappeared from summer homes. Hunger didn't hurt him as much as loneliness. No one petted him, no one held him, no one even ever said hello. He trotted along the streets of town like a ghost dog, unrecognized, unapproached. After a while, he noticed that all the other dogs kept their owners on a leash, and Snix didn't blame them. If he had someone who loved him, he'd want to be permanently connected, too.

During the days, as he hunted through the town for something, anything, to eat, he couldn't help catching sight of what he was pretty sure was himself in the shop windows. He was scrawny, with ribs curving beneath tangled matted hair. It was embarrassing.

No wonder the girl had left him behind.

It encouraged him slightly when locals began to put up lights all over their houses and the town lined the streets with fragrant green trees covered in small glittering bulbs. Frigid air blew over the island, but more visitors kept arriving, gabbing away with their hands clutching hot cups of coffee, munching heavenly-scented sweet rolls, dropping the occasional crumb that Snix tried to get to after the people walked away, before the seagulls swooped in.

He was surviving. It was worse when the blowing rain or snow began. Back porches provided little shelter, so he huddled, shivering, inside bushes or beneath cars. In the daylight, what little there was of it, he ran through the streets, searching for food and a warmer spot.

He was so lonely.

6

❄

"Know what, Mommy?" Kennedy grumbled. "I hate this season."

"I never liked it, either," Katya sympathized.

"It's such a *bother*." Kennedy was reclining on her mother's living room sofa, visiting for the afternoon. Alonzo had taken Maddox down to the condo's gym to play, which almost made Kennedy like the man, even if her mother had run off with him. Kennedy could still hope with all her heart that her mother would come to her senses and return to her father.

"All the awful parties," Katya agreed. "It's so hard not to gain weight."

Kennedy cast a skeptical eye at her mother, who hadn't gained an ounce after her twenty-fifth birthday.

Katya had learned to slenderize her body and her life before it became all the rage. She always chose modern furniture with sleek, clean lines. She hated clutter. She disdained "collectibles." Her clothing, too, was classic. No ruffles, no lace, no faux anything. White shirts and khakis in the summer, white cashmere turtleneck sweaters and khakis in the winter. Black dresses for evening wear. Real pearls. Costume jewelry—ugh. Only real, large—but not vulgar—diamond solitaires for her ears. Her blond hair was always cut to fall just to her chin, sweeping from a side part.

"How do you stay so skinny?" Kennedy asked.

"Exercise and willpower," Katya told her. "Your weight has to be your first priority in life. It's extremely hard work. I'll admit I've suffered at times."

"But it's worth it, right, Mom? I mean, just look at you."

Katya preened. "Thank you, darling."

"I'll lose weight after I have the baby."

"Of course you will."

Kennedy made a face. "But we've got to go to Dad's next Sunday for the whole *week*!"

"It will be fine," Katya assured her daughter. "Come on. This way, Nicole has to do all the fussing about Christmas. She'll do all the cooking and cleaning. You won't have to do a thing. Sebastian will take care of Maddox. He and James can go off and do manly things. You'll be able to rest."

"I hope so, because you know Nicole is going to fill

Maddox with candy and icing. He'll be a hyperactive monkey boy."

"What are you getting Nicole for Christmas?" Katya sipped from her mug of unsweetened green tea and settled more comfortably into her chrome and leather chair.

Kennedy shrugged. "I have no idea. I've only met her once. I don't know what that woman likes."

"Get her some chocolates." Katya leered wickedly over the top of her mug.

Kennedy giggled. "You are bad." Nicole wasn't fat, exactly, but she didn't have Katya's lean, lithe lines.

"Why?" Katya widened her eyes innocently. "All women like chocolates."

Kennedy snorted. "Nicole obviously does."

"Don't be mean, Kennedy. My sources tell me Nicole is a very nice woman, and your father seems satisfied enough with her."

"Oh, Mommy!" Kennedy struggled to sit up. "Why'd you have to leave Daddy?"

"Darling, we've been over this before. Your father and I were boring together. You are grown and married. It was right for me to have some ME in my life."

Kennedy flopped back against the pillows. "By ME, you mean Alonzo. Sex."

Katya rolled her eyes and directed the subject back to the holidays. "So. You can order chocolates for Nicole online. Go Godiva, that's always easy and best. Send her the biggest box. They'll gift wrap it. *Done*. For your father, go online and order a few of the newest biographies. You know all the man does is read." Katya yawned. "SO boring."

"Mommy." Kennedy didn't like her parents criticizing each other.

"What did you get James?"

"Nothing yet." Kennedy poked her enormous belly. "Maybe I'll order him a life-size blow-up doll he can have sex with."

Katya ignored this. "Does he need a new golf bag? Tennis whites?"

"For Christmas? In New England? We can't go anywhere, may I remind you, because this baby boy is coming in January. So, no Florida, no Aruba, just snow."

"Now let's be positive. How about cross-country skis for James and for Maddox? They can go out together."

"That's a good idea. I've ordered a sled from L.L. Bean for Maddox." Kennedy gazed around the living room. No tree, no pines on the fireplace mantel, no presents. "What are you doing for Christmas?"

"I told you, Kennedy. Where is your mind these days? Alonzo and I are going to a cleansing spa in Switzerland for ten days. No fats, no alcohol, no sugar. Lots of exercise and fresh air. Indoor tennis, of course."

"You told me you were going to a spa, but you didn't say Switzerland!" Kennedy sat up, alarmed. "Mommy, what about the baby?"

"Kennedy, he's not due until the middle of January. I'll be back on December thirtieth. Plenty of time."

"You've got to be!" Kennedy ran her hands over her belly. "I need you there, and Daddy and James."

"We'll do our best."

"I know you will. Still—"

"Ssh. It's going to be fine." Katya glanced at her watch. "I've got my yoga class in about thirty minutes . . ."

"I know. I should get Maddox home for his dinner, anyway." Kennedy pushed her arms back, trying to extract herself from the sofa.

Katya watched her daughter with an assessing eye. "I promised to give you money for a nanny."

"I know, Mommy, and I'm grateful. But I want to bond with the new baby, even if he is a boy."

"It's a shame about that. Girls' clothes are so much cuter. But never mind, Kennedy, it will be fun for Maddox to have a brother to play with."

Kennedy had achieved a standing position. "I wish James would take a week's vacation and spend it with me and the new baby, and especially with Maddox. It would be wonderful for Maddox to have his father give him special attention when we have a new baby."

"James has an important job with his brokerage firm, Kennedy. You're being far too idealistic with this bonding mumbo-jumbo. Get a nanny, let her care for the baby, and *you* spend time with Maddox. I had a nanny for you, and you turned out all right."

Kennedy lumbered across the room and into the hall. She pressed the intercom and told Alonzo that he should bring Maddox up.

"Maddox wants a puppy," she said over her shoulder to her mother. "I told him no. I can't deal with a puppy and a new baby. Plus, I'm allergic to animals."

"Are you, darling? I never knew that."

Kennedy stared at her mother. "I thought that was why we never had a pet."

"Oh? I must have forgotten." Katya opened the closet door and took out Maddox's little black dress coat and wool cap. She handed them to Kennedy. "I'm sure you're right."

7

❄

It was the middle of December. Nicole wore a blue roll-neck cotton pullover with a large white snowflake in the center. She'd opened her holiday jewelry box and selected snowflake earrings to match. They'd cost less than five dollars and were iridescent—she could still remember how pleased she was to discover them at a local pharmacy. She looked pretty cute, even if she did say so herself. Kennedy, of course, would consider her sweater sappy. But Kennedy wasn't here yet.

And today they were going to buy the tree!

They bundled up in puffy down coats and leather gloves and drove out of town to Moors End Farm on Polpis Road.

Snow wasn't falling, but the wind blew fiercely, and overhead the sky hung low and white, as if ready to drop its load of flakes at any moment. Sebastian squeezed the car between two others. He and Nicole slammed their car doors and leaned into the wind, battling toward the trees propped against wooden supports.

Nicole headed toward the tallest trees. After a moment, she noticed Sebastian was no longer beside her. He'd stalked over to the area with the midget trees.

"Sebastian!" she called. "Over here!"

Sebastian waved to her, indicating that she should come over to where he stood.

"No!" Nicole called. "Tall!" She raised her arms high and wide. "BIG!"

Sebastian hurried over to her, looking worried. "Nicole, we don't have the decorations or the lights for such a large tree."

Nicole wriggled cheekily. "*I* do. I brought a couple of boxes when I moved here. Plus, we can buy more lights in a flash!"

Sebastian chuckled at her weak joke. "I'm afraid I'm not much help with all this tree business."

"You'll be all the help I need when you carry it into the house," Nicole assured him.

A burly sales clerk in a red-checked flannel jacket and a fuzzy green hat appeared.

"What about this one?" he suggested, pulling out an eight-foot-tall tree and shaking it so its branches fell away a bit from their tightly twined position.

"Look, Seb, it's *flawless*." Nicole clapped her hands in

delight. She'd never seen such a sublime evergreen. "It's shaped like an A. Each side is bushy, so we won't have to tuck one bad side in a corner to hide it."

Sebastian glanced fondly at his wife, who was practically levitating in her pleasure. "Okay," he surrendered. "This tree."

At the small shed where they paid, Nicole bought a wreath for the front door, too. A *tasteful* wreath with a large red bow and nothing else, no small decorations, no candy canes, no pine cones dusted with faux snow, which she would have preferred. This was her private concession to Sebastian's decorous (lackluster) tastes. While he and Katya had never had a Christmas tree in the house, Nicole couldn't imagine Christmas without one.

With the lumberjack's help, Sebastian easily hefted the tree to the top of his SUV and fastened it with rope and bungee cords.

Getting it into the house was a different matter entirely. The tree was heavy. Sebastian removed the cords and wrestled it to the ground, but once he'd gotten his hands on the trunk, he had trouble lifting it and for a moment stumbled around the car as if dancing with a clumsy drunk in a green fir coat.

Nicole stifled a giggle. "Let me take the top to guide it in." She stuck her hands in between the branches, grabbed the slender trunk, and together they carried it into the living room. They dropped it on the floor, then wrestled it into the stand Nicole had placed in readiness.

Sebastian stood back, staring at the tree. "It's awfully big."

"I know," Nicole agreed smugly. She cocked her head, studying her husband. "Tell you what. If you'll help me put the lights on, I'll do the rest of the decorating."

His posture relaxed. "That's a deal. I was hoping to meet the guys for lunch at Downyflake."

After they strung the lights on the evergreen, Sebastian walked into town to meet his friends. Nicole brought out her beloved old ornaments, set them on the floor, and evaluated them. She was in a new stage of her life, this was the biggest tree she'd ever had, and she wanted it to be the most glorious. She hurried into her car and drove to Marine Home Center.

In the housewares section of the shop, "White Christmas" played softly over the sound system. Christmas baubles filled the shelves, each more adorable than the other. Mothers with children knelt down to discuss which miniature crèche scene to purchase for their houses. Honestly, the ornaments became cleverer every year, Nicole thought, in a frenzy of confusion over how to limit herself to just a few choices. Penguins on ice skates, red-nosed reindeer, trains with wheels like red and white peppermint candy, airplanes with Snoopy waving and his red scarf flying backward, snowflakes, grinning camels, tiny dolls in white velvet coats with red berries in their hair . . . Oh, Nicole *loved* this season!

She bought lots of decorations, and if she thought she might be going just a wee bit overboard, she remembered Maddox. What fun it would be to have a child in the house for Christmas!

Back home, she listened to a holiday CD while she hung the ornaments. As she worked, she discovered she needed to rearrange the furniture, to push the sofas and chairs away from the tall, bushy tree. Standing back, she wondered if it wasn't just a bit overwhelming. Had she made a mistake? Misjudged? Was the tree too big? Was she just a hopeless cornball with no sense of restraint and elegance?

She resisted hanging one last candy cane, plugged in the small multi-colored lights, and collapsed on the sofa to review her handiwork. It was quite an amazing sight, she thought, bright, joyful, playful . . . absentmindedly she chewed on the end of the candy cane. Oh! She was hungry! She'd worked right through lunch. No wonder she had misgivings about the tree. Her blood sugar was low.

Or was the tree *too much*? Would Sebastian's heart sink when he saw it, would he realize with horror that the woman he married lacked all sense of refinement? Nicole worriedly crunched the candy cane.

"I'm home!" Sebastian's voice boomed out as he came in the door, bringing a blast of cold winter air with him.

Nicole glanced up nervously. "Did you have a nice lunch?"

Sebastian strode across the room, pulled her to her feet, and kissed her soundly.

"My," she sighed. "What's that for?"

"That's for the tree," Sebastian told her. "You should come out and see it from the street. It's great. I've never seen anything like it."

She laughed with pleasure. "It's not too big for this room?"

He studied it. "It's big. It's so big it reminds me of the trees my parents used to put up when I was a little boy." His face softened. "So long ago."

"Oh, you've still got a bit of little boy in you," Nicole teased him, nuzzling his neck.

Sebastian grinned. "Don't you mean big boy?" he joked.

"Why, Sebastian." She hugged him, turning her head sideways to gaze at the tree, feeling warm and loved and smug and absolutely brimming with holiday spirit.

8

❄

The ferry from Hyannis to Nantucket was like a game of bump-'em cars Maddox once had been on at a friend's birthday party. The big boat raised up, then smashed down, and waves slammed into the giant boat's hull, making it shudder. Maddox thought it was *awesome*.

His mommy didn't like it much, though. She lay on a bench, wrapped in her coat, hands clutching her belly.

"Let's go up top, Mad Man," James said, taking his son by the hand.

This was awesome, too. Maddox rarely got alone time with his daddy, who was always working. Maddox felt secure with his tiny hand tucked inside Daddy's large warm hand. They went up the stairs, taking care because of the heaving boat, and stood by the high windows looking out at the water. His daddy lifted him up into his arms so Maddox could see better, and Maddox inhaled deeply of his daddy's masculine scent, his aftershave lotion, his wool sweater, his cotton turtleneck. Maddox wrapped one arm around his father's neck and leaned against him slightly, so he could feel the raspy skin on his face.

"Maybe we'll see a whale out here," his daddy said.

"How do they stay warm?" Maddox asked.

James explained, "The animals and fish that live in the water have different bodies from human beings. They can breathe in the water, and they never get cold. But they can't breathe in the air like we do, and our air is much too dry for them."

Maddox marveled at this thought. He gazed out into the waves, which were dark blue, crested with frothy white, rolling relentlessly toward the boat to crash into the sides, making the boat shiver and the waves explode into fizzy silver suds.

He tightened his hold on his father. The world was so big, and this view of it on such a cold December day made him feel very small. In preschool, he'd seen a picture book depicting Santa Claus traveling to an island in his sleigh. The sleigh was drawn by porpoises, seals, walruses, and whales, and it skipped over the top of the waves while Santa held the reins.

The book had made Maddox uneasy. Santa was supposed to fly through the air. Maddox had seen pictures of the sleigh in other books. What did Santa do with the reindeer when he used the porpoises? And if he crossed the water with the sea creatures, what happened when he got to the island? If what his father said was right, porpoises couldn't breathe on dry land, so how did Santa get up to the chimneys of the houses? It was hard to understand how the world worked, especially on an island.

A funny *yip* interrupted Maddox's thoughts. Looking down, he saw a yellow puppy tugging the laces of his daddy's sneakers.

A lady with gray hair and earrings shaped like Christmas trees rushed over. "I'm so sorry," she apologized pleasantly. She picked up the puppy and held him in her arms. "This is Chips," she told Maddox and his father. Holding the puppy's paw, she waved it in a hello gesture. "We're taking Chips to give to our granddaughter for Christmas." Seeing Maddox's face, she asked, "Would you like to pet him?"

Maddox nodded solemnly.

"I'll put him on the floor. You can play with him. Be careful, he bites, well, not actually *bites*, he nibbles, he's got his baby teeth, and he's only two months old. He doesn't mean to hurt."

James set Maddox down on the floor next to the puppy. Maddox held out his hand. Chips licked it and wriggled all over. Maddox patted the puppy, then scratched behind his ears. Chips turned circles and flopped over onto his back, exposing his fat white belly. Maddox rubbed it and Chips wiggled in ecstasy, kicking his hind legs as if he were riding a bike. Maddox giggled.

"Here." The lady handed Maddox a short rope. "He loves to tug."

The second Maddox took the rope, Chips snatched the other end in his sharp white puppy teeth and yanked so hard he pulled it right out of Maddox's hand.

"Hey!" Maddox yelled, reaching out to capture the rope, but Chips ran away. Giggling, Maddox chased after him. They went only a few steps when Chips tripped on his own feet and somersaulted head over heels, never once letting go of the rope. But Maddox caught up with him and clutched the rope, and the boy and the puppy began to tug. It was so much fun. Maddox laughed and laughed. The puppy let go of the rope and actually jumped onto Maddox, who was on his knees. Chips sort of latched onto Maddox with his puppy paws and began licking Maddox's face all over, as if Maddox tasted delicious. Maddox fell over on his back, delirious with happiness as the puppy's wet pink tongue slurped his eyelids, his cheeks, and once right up his nose!

"Maddox, darling? Why are you on the floor?" His mommy stood at the top of the stairs, clutching the railing, pale and anxious. "Are you all right?"

The older lady quickly bent down and lifted Chips off Maddox. "Hello," she said to Kennedy. "I'm sorry, I was just letting Chips play with the child. I'm afraid I'm rather boring for the poor puppy."

His mommy smiled. "That's so kind of you. Maddox would love to have a puppy. I'm just not sure I could deal with one now . . ." She put her hand on her belly.

The older lady nodded her head. "Wiser to take your time. You can always get a puppy later."

Maddox glanced back and forth between the older woman and his mommy, who seemed to be communicating without saying all the words.

James hefted Maddox into his arms. "Look," he said, pointing. "We're almost there. I see the lighthouse. Soon we'll be nice and warm, and Nicole will serve us a delicious meal."

"Goodbye," the woman said, waving Chips's paw.

Maddox's daddy said, "Kennedy, let me help you go back down the stairs. You shouldn't have climbed them by yourself, not with the boat rocking so much."

Supporting Maddox with one arm, and Maddox's mommy with the other, his strong daddy carefully escorted them down the steps to the main cabin. They were almost on the island!

9

❄

Kennedy was so blissed-out she was miserable.

After their arrival yesterday afternoon, her father had helped James carry in the bags. To Kennedy's surprise, the room at the back of the house behind the kitchen had been transformed into a bedroom. This way, Nicole had pointed out, Kennedy wouldn't have to climb the stairs. The room had been called the birthing room when the house was built back in the eighteen hundreds, because it was near the kitchen and easy to keep warm. When her parents were married, this room was the TV room.

Kennedy had worried that Maddox would be afraid to be on the second floor, so far away from his parents, but Nicole had decorated the spare bedroom in a spaceship theme, with posters of rockets and a bedspread printed with comets. All around the ceiling, small stickers of stars, planets, and meteors glowed gently in the dark. A bookshelf held building blocks, children's books, and tractors, dump trucks, and fire engines. Maddox loved it. He immediately called it *his* room.

Last night, Nicole had served a delicious meal, even though the calorie count was over the moon. Pork loin with apples and onions, roasted squash risotto, broccolini, beets with orange sauce, and fresh, homemade, whole wheat bread with butter. She'd bought the kind of veggie burgers Kennedy had requested and cooked those for Maddox, who ate all of them, as well as his broccolini and beets.

This morning, Nicole and Kennedy's father had taken Maddox out for breakfast in town, allowing Kennedy and James to sleep late and spend time alone in bed snuggling, something they had been unable to do for months.

Then, because the day was sunny and surprisingly mild, her father and Nicole had suggested having a picnic way out on Great Point, where Maddox could see the lighthouse and the big fat seals who lounged about on the shore, grunting, lolling, and snorting.

The last thing Kennedy wanted to do was to be bounced around in a four-wheel-drive vehicle along a sandy beach path. Her lower back was twinging with such force she felt like a grunting seal herself.

When she begged off going, to her utter amazement, Nicole had cooed, "Of course you should stay home. Why don't you settle on the sofa? I'll have your father build you a nice fire. I've got a stack of magazines and light reading you might enjoy. Go on, put your feet up. Get comfy."

Kennedy had lowered her bulk onto the sofa and raised her heavy feet up to a pillow. Instant ecstasy. Before she left, Nicole brought in a tray. On it were a plate of sandwiches, a bowl of carrots and red pepper strips, and to Kennedy's childish delight, a selection of homemade Christmas cookies. Gingerbread men and women with white icing faces. Irresistible sugar cookies with snowy icing covered with multicolored sprinkles shaped like reindeer, wreaths, and angels. Finally—in a white pot decorated with green holly and red berries—there was steaming, rich, milky, homemade hot chocolate to pour into a matching mug.

Kennedy's father, James, and Maddox were hefting a picnic basket, several wool blankets, and a couple of thermoses out to the Jeep Grand Cherokee.

"Bye, Mommy," Maddox called.

Nicole came back into the living room, wearing jeans, a green Christmas sweater with a snowman on it, and hiking boots. "All set?" In her hands she held a red and green plaid down blanket trimmed in satin. "I'll just tuck this in around you." She fluttered the cover over Kennedy's legs and nudged it in around Kennedy's feet. She scooted the coffee table close, just within Kennedy's reach. "Anything else?"

"This is great," Kennedy admitted grudgingly. "Thank you."

"Bye, then. See you in a few hours." Nicole fluttered her fingers and left.

A few hours? A few hours alone in the house with cookies, hot chocolate, and peace and quiet? Kennedy almost wept with relief.

Although . . . something about being tucked in with a blanket unsettled her, brought up memories from the far distant past that filled her with a melancholy longing. Now she was the one who made sure her child was covered with a blanket, but there had been times, she could almost remember, like reaching out through a fog, when her own mother had fluttered a blanket down over her.

Katya hadn't ever cared much for the messiness of motherhood. She'd always had babysitters, or nannies, and of course, housekeepers. Kennedy's father was always working. From an early age, Kennedy was encouraged to be a good girl, a "big girl"—meaning no fussing, no running, no whining.

Kennedy worried that she wasn't a natural mother. She never felt the rush of exultation when Maddox was born that she'd read other mothers had. True, she'd had an epidural, which Katya had advised her to have, in order to avoid the pain of labor and birth that, Katya said, would savage Kennedy. Even with an epidural, Kennedy was shattered for days, which stretched into weeks and months. When Maddox was about seven months old, he started sleeping all night, and after that Kennedy very nearly felt like a normal human being. But when he started crawling and toddling, her fears for him, the need for constant vigilance, the shrieks he sent out when he fell, wiped her out all over again.

She loved him more than her life. He was her joy, her angel, her darling boy. After he was a bit more steady, she and Maddox had entered a kind of honeymoon period, when they had such fun together. He was her darling pal.

It was during that spell when she submitted to James's desire for another child. She had prayed for a girl, but the ultrasound tech said it was another boy. Kennedy tried to be content with that. Certainly it made James feel manly, as if every cell in his body was masculine.

This pregnancy had been as difficult as the first. Morning sickness came early and lasted for months, spiraling nausea through her system day and night. Even though she scarcely ate, the baby grew inside her as if her umbilical cord were an enormous beanstalk attached to a giant. She was uncomfortable, awkward, blotchy, waddly, and incontinent. *Cranky.*

Now she had this dreadful week to get through with

her father and his new gushy wife. Nicole had never had children, she probably had no idea of the difficulties of keeping a four-year-old boy amused and under control. Kennedy was terrified that Nicole would feed Maddox so much sugar he'd never sleep. Plus, the environment Nicole had provided—the huge tree, the toy crèche, the stockings hanging from the mantel—they would overstimulate her already active son, causing him to spin out of control.

Kennedy wanted to go home. She wanted this Christmas fuss to be over and done with. She wanted Maddox back in preschool and her days quiet and calm, so she could sleep and rest up for the coming baby.

Although, Kennedy admitted to herself as she poured a cup of hot chocolate and nibbled a sugar cookie, this wasn't so bad. Pretty nice, actually.

So, fine. Nicole was obviously doing her best. That didn't mean that Kennedy had to like her or be glad that her father had gone and *married* her.

Why couldn't her father understand that women had midlife crises just like men? Obviously, Katya had been bored with her husband of thirty years and had just needed some excitement. Perhaps Katya was beginning to feel—not *old*, Katya would never be old—but less alluring than usual. After all, Katya's daughter was grown up and married now, and Katya had become a *grandmother* with its connotations of gray hair in a bun and flapping upper arms. Kennedy totally *knew* her mother had run off with Alonzo to prove to herself that she was still desirable. Instead of divorcing Katya, Kennedy's father should have gone after her, wooed her, and won her back. He still could, if he hadn't married that damned Nicole.

What was so great about Nicole, anyway, that Sebastian had to marry her? She was pretty, but not beautiful like Katya, and she was, okay, not fat, but definitely plump. She wasn't classy, couldn't play tennis or sail, didn't know any of Sebastian's friends. Why couldn't Kennedy's father just have had a frivolous fling with her and then gotten back together with Katya?

Maybe he still could.

Maybe this week could illuminate for Sebastian how awful it was to be without his beautiful, sophisticated, silky ex-wife.

Maybe Kennedy could demonstrate to her father how hard it was for her to be in this house, her mother's house really, with Nicole the Interloper, and Sebastian would be overcome with guilt for marrying Nicole, and divorce her and remarry Katya!

This would take some cunning on Kennedy's part.

Kennedy ate another gingerbread cookie. She finished

her mug of hot chocolate. She reached for a magazine, relaxed back against the cushions, and read about the loves of Hollywood celebrities and pregnancies of princesses until her eyes drifted closed and a soft slumber possessed her.

10

❄

Nicole sat in the backseat with Maddox during the long bumpy ride out to Great Point. Seb's Jeep Grand Cherokee easily churned through the deep sand, tossing the passengers up and down, which made Maddox shriek with glee. The day was full of wind and surf and clouds blowing over the sun, sending a glancing, dancing brilliant light across the beach and into their eyes.

Sebastian stopped the Jeep near the lighthouse. Only a few yards away, scores of harbor seals lounged on the sand.

Maddox giggled as they stepped out onto the beach. "I want to pet one," he told his daddy.

"Darling, they bite," Nicole warned. "You can't go near them. They're wild creatures."

They strolled the beach, picking up shells, staying far away from the winter waves crashing on the shore. Nearby, a clan of the larger horsehead seals bobbed in the water like a gang of curious wet gorillas. James lifted Maddox up on his shoulders so the boy could see a fishing boat anchored in the distance, among the white-capped waves.

"I'm hungry!" Maddox declared.

"Then let's eat," Nicole replied easily.

Sitting on a picnic blanket, they munched lunch while watching the seals, who muttered and oinked like sea pigs. At one point, two seals got into a snorting argument, a comic scene that made everyone laugh.

After lunch, they walked through the dunes up to the sixty-foot-high, whitewashed stone lighthouse. They returned to the Jeep and bumped back down the sand to the area called Coskata, where to Maddox's great delight, they spotted a snowy owl, pristine white and immensely arrogant, seated on a scrub oak. They tromped through a wooded glade to find Nicole's favorite tree, an ancient beech with arms stretching out like elephants' trunks. It was perfect for climbing, so Maddox scrambled up onto one of the lower branches, and Sebastian took his photo. They continued on the narrow path until they arrived at a pond where a white heron stalked among the marshy grasses. Maddox helped Nicole fill a bucket with mussels they picked from the shoreline and they scampered about on a fallen tree trunk. Sebastian led them to a midden, a gathering of broken shells left from a long-ago Native American tribe. He told Maddox about how the early

Americans had lived here, eating fish and berries, drinking water from the ponds, covered with goose grease in the summer to protect them from mosquito bites. Maddox's eyes went wide with amazement.

In the late afternoon, when the sun was beginning to set, Sebastian steered the SUV off the sand and onto the paved road leading back to town. He yawned. Beside him, in the passenger seat, James yawned. In the backseat, both Nicole and Maddox caught the contagious reflex and yawned so hard they squeaked.

"Close your eyes," Nicole urged Maddox. "Take a nap."

The boy didn't need to be invited twice. He sagged into his rented car seat and was immediately asleep.

So much fresh air and exercise. Nicole leaned her head back against the seat and closed her own eyes, congratulating herself for having prepared a casserole for their dinner tonight. She'd steam the mussels for a first course with melted butter, but that would take only a few minutes. She hoped Kennedy had had a restful day and would be pleased by Nicole's efforts.

Sebastian brought the Jeep to a stop by the two air pumps stationed by the side of the road just past the Trustees of Reservations cabin. He took the tire pressure gauge out of the glove compartment. Air had to be let out of the tires for easy driving on the sand, and Maddox had been fascinated by the way his grandfather made the air hiss out by pressing a rock on the valve stem. Nicole wasn't surprised when Maddox sprang awake from his light doze.

"Want to help me put the air back in?" Sebastian asked his grandson.

Maddox eagerly unfastened his seat belt and jumped out of the car. James filled the tires on the right side, Sebastian and Maddox took the ones on the left. Then they buckled up and drove away toward town.

Back at the house, Nicole was delighted to discover Kennedy with rosy cheeks and bright eyes.

"Thank you, Daddy." Kennedy waddled up to Sebastian and gave him a hug. "I had the best rest I've had in weeks."

Nicole waited for Kennedy to thank her, too. Instead, Kennedy squatted down, bracing herself with one hand on a wall, to hug Maddox.

"Did you have fun, honey-bunny?"

"Mommy, I saw seals! And a rabbit! And an owl! And I put air in a tire!" Maddox was almost stammering with excitement.

"Tell me all about it in the bath," Kennedy suggested. She held out a hand and her husband hoisted her to her feet. "I'll take Maddox up for a nice long bath. You guys can enjoy drinks before dinner."

With her son yammering away, Kennedy slowly went up the stairs.

Nicole carried the bucket of mussels into the kitchen, trying not to mind that Kennedy had not even bothered to say hello to her. She set the bucket in the sink, washed her hands, and went into the living room to gather up the plate of cookies and the hot chocolate. The cookies, she noticed, had disappeared. The magazines were scattered over the floor. The blanket was balled up, hanging half over the arm of the sofa. Crumbs littered the sofa and the carpet, as well as a used napkin and a few used tissues.

At the sight of the tissues wadded up on the floor, Nicole sat down with a sigh and took a moment to compose herself.

Really? she thought. Did Kennedy expect Nicole not only to provide all the meals and snacks, but also to pick up after her like a servant? True, Kennedy was bulky with her pregnancy, but she was standing up when they arrived home. Surely Kennedy could have carried her used tissues into the waste basket in the bathroom. Sebastian had told Nicole what a neat freak Katya was, and Nicole was certain Katya had passed along her tidiness to Kennedy, so this clutter Kennedy had left was more than a mess—it was a message.

I don't like you, and I never will. Was that the point of the lumpy tissues, the strewn magazines? What on earth had Nicole done to warrant such animosity? She knew Kennedy wanted her parents to get back together, but Kennedy was not demented, she had to realize her mother had been hooked up with the gorgeous Alonzo for years.

Nicole gathered up the magazines and patted them into a neat pile on the coffee table. With thumb and forefinger, she pinched up the used tissues and napkin and dropped them on the tray next to the empty cookie plate, mug, and pot. Nicole was slow to anger, but she was on her way now. She took a moment to feast her eyes on the Christmas tree, trying to absorb its gleaming serenity into her mood.

She had never had children, but she believed that if Kennedy were her child, she would confront her. She would scold her. At the least, she would force Kennedy to recognize her existence and her attempts to make this a pleasant holiday for everyone.

Sebastian stuck his head into the room. "James and I are going to have a drink. Could I fix you one?"

Nicole relaxed her gritted teeth. "A glass of red wine would be excellent right now," she replied. Perhaps that would calm her down, put her back in the Christmas spirit, and prevent her from doing or saying something she would later regret.

11

❄

Maddox woke early, as he always did. He played with the cool toys in his room as quietly as he could, because his mommy needed her sleep for the baby. He looked at the picture books. He stood at the window staring out at Granddad's backyard. It was kind of interesting, with its toolshed and wooden picnic table and benches. If he tipped over the benches, and maybe if he could find a big cardboard box, he could make a fort like his friend Jeremy had. Cool!

He trotted out of his room, down the stairs, through the hall to the kitchen and the mudroom with the back door.

"Going somewhere, sport?" Granddad sat at the kitchen table with a cup of coffee and a newspaper.

Nicole was at the other end of the table, drinking coffee and making a list on a pad of paper. They were both wearing pajamas, robes, and furry slippers.

Maddox requested, politely, "May I please play in the backyard?"

"I don't see why not," Granddad answered.

"Hang on," said Nicole. "You need to get dressed first, Maddox. You'll freeze in your pajamas. Have you been to the bathroom yet?"

Maddox slumped. He'd thought Nicole was different, but she was just like the other adults, full of rules.

Nicole rose from the table and held out her hand. "Let me help you get dressed. I'll pick out your warmest pants."

Maddox stared at the door to the room where his mommy and daddy slept.

"We won't wake your parents," Nicole whispered. "We'll be quiet as two little mice."

She was as good as her word. She tiptoed with Maddox up the stairs. They didn't speak as she helped him dress and use the bathroom. They went like pirates back down the stairs, and no one woke up.

In the kitchen, Nicole asked, "Want some breakfast before you go outside, Maddox?"

"No, thank you. I want to make a fort out of the picnic table and benches." He thought he might as well just come out with the truth in case they didn't like that sort of thing, their yard getting all messed up.

Nicole surprised him. "Good idea. We've got some folding lawn chairs in the shed that will make a good doorway on the ends. I'll get them out for you after I get dressed."

Maddox eyed her skeptically. He wasn't sure about those lawn chairs. He wasn't sure he wanted his idea tampered with.

"Boots," Nicole said. "Coat, cap, and mittens." She retrieved the items from the hooks in the mudroom and put them on Maddox, a cumbersome process he hated. He was never cold and the extra padding made it harder to move. But he allowed himself to be yanked, tugged, and zipped, because he understood the adults were right.

Finally, Nicole unlocked the back door. Maddox stepped onto the back porch.

"Stay in the backyard, now, Maddox," Nicole warned. "Don't go away, promise?"

"I promise."

The back porch was like a room without walls. It had a swing hanging from the ceiling, and a wicker sofa and two wicker armchairs. The wide steps going down had railings on each side. Maddox hung on to them as he went, his slightly-too-big boots hampering him, making him clumsy.

The backyard was bordered by a fence and also by hedges with stubborn green-brown leaves hanging on to the brown twiggy branches. He could see where flowers had been in the summer, because the beds were edged with shells. A white birdbath stood at the other end of the yard. He ran through the brown grass to check—it had water in it, and a black feather. He picked out the feather and put it in his pocket. Returning to the flower beds bordering the lawn, he spent some time checking out the shells. Most were white, with pale purple streaks on the inside. Some had tips sharp enough to cut, others were rolled up like burritos. Here and there green or blue sea glass twinkled, edges smoothed to satin by the ocean waves.

A hawthorn tree grew at the end of the garden. It had a few red berries left. Nicole told him the birds liked the berries, so he liked the tree, even though its thorns made it impossible to climb.

It *was* cold out. He looked up and up, at the sky. It was white, heavy, and damp-looking, like a wet pillow. Maybe it would snow. He hoped so. His mommy said he'd seen snow before, but he couldn't remember. If it did snow, his fort would be a perfect place to keep warm, so he stomped over to the picnic table and benches.

It took him a few tries to wrestle the bench over so it was lying on its side, legs sticking out, the long flat seat side acting like a wall. He stomped around to the other side and struggled to tip the other bench over. Finally he succeeded. He went to one end of the table and crawled under.

It wasn't much of a fort. The seats of the benches didn't come all the way up to the table top, so a long space was exposed on each side. The dry grass was crackly. He sat for a moment, considering what kind of fort it should be. Pirate? Spaceship? Indian?

A door opened. Nicole stepped out onto the porch, wearing a navy blue sweater with ice-skating penguins slipping and twirling all over it. The sweater made him laugh.

"Penguins don't ice-skate!" he called.

Nicole came down the steps. "Oh, I wouldn't be so sure." She headed toward the shed at the back of the garden and yanked the door open. "Let's see what we've got for you."

Maddox raced over to peer inside the dark enclosure. Reaching up, Nicole pulled a chain, and a light came on, a single bulb hanging from the ceiling. The building was wonderful, with a slate floor, high work benches along two walls, shelves along the third, and yard implements leaning on the fourth. He saw rakes, a lawn mower, shovels, saws. Coiled onto a special rack was a green garden hose. Pots, paint cans, and other containers sat on the shelves. Above them, outlined in white chalk, were the tools: hammers, pliers, wrenches, screwdrivers. He wanted to get them down and *do* something.

Nicole said, "Look, here: the folding lawn chairs I told

you about. See?" Picking up an aluminum chair with webbed seat and back, she opened it, and turned it sideways, to display how it could be used as a wall.

Maddox nodded. "Cool."

"Shall we take them out?"

Maddox nodded again.

Nicole hoisted two chairs, one under each arm. Maddox took a third chair, which was surprisingly lightweight, holding it as well as he could in front of him, following Nicole back to the picnic table. Returning to the shed, Nicole reached up to lift a couple of fat vinyl cushions from a shelf.

"These might be good as seats in your fort," she told him.

Maddox grinned. "Oh, yeah."

She tossed him one and carried two out herself. She dropped them outside the fort, seeming to understand how private the enterprise was to him. He wanted to arrange things himself, even if it took him time and struggle.

Back in the shed, Nicole stood with her hands on her hips and scanned the walls. "Let's see. What else?" Cocking her head, she suggested, "What about these?"

She handed him a pair of field glasses. Puzzled, he turned them around in his hands. Nicole knelt down and demonstrated how to use them. She helped him turn the round knob until the view went clear.

Maddox was speechless. This was the most excellent fort toy he had ever seen. He raced away, binoculars in hand, ready to enter his fantasy world.

12

❄

Nicole returned to the kitchen, shivering slightly. She'd gone out to the shed without a coat or hat and the day was frosty.

Sebastian rose from the table. "I'll get shaved and dressed and bring in more firewood." He smacked a kiss on her lips.

Nicole poured her second cup of coffee and stood at the window, keeping an eye on Maddox as he dragged a floral cushion from the shed to his fort. Hearing a shuffling noise, she turned to see Kennedy coming into the kitchen, wrapped in a puffy pink robe that couldn't quite close over her belly.

"Good morning, Kennedy," Nicole said brightly.

Kennedy collapsed in a chair. "I hope you've got bacon and eggs for breakfast. I'm starved."

Nicole stared. She counted to ten. She recalled her years on the wards as a nurse, when patients were too ill to be polite, unable to do more than mumble. Kennedy was only pregnant, not sick, but still, this was a state Nicole had never endured, so she decided to be kind.

"I'll be glad to make you some, Kennedy," Nicole offered.

Kennedy buried her face in her hands.

Alarmed, Nicole came closer to the table. "Kennedy, do you feel all right?"

Kennedy didn't raise her head. "I told you. I'm hungry."

Without another word, Nicole set about microwaving bacon and scrambling eggs. She shaved slivers of cheddar into the eggs and added a pinch of basil. She squeezed oranges and set a fresh glass of juice in front of Kennedy. She placed a napkin and utensils near Kennedy's place.

She had to admit, Kennedy had stamina. Nicole could never sit in steaming silence while another woman cooked for her.

Gosh. Maybe Kennedy was truly ill. Worry spurted into Nicole's chest.

"Good morning, gorgeous!" James came out of the guest bedroom, smelling of soap and aftershave. "Morning, Nicole."

"Hi, James. Would you like some eggs and bacon? I'm fixing some for Kennedy."

To Nicole's delighted surprise, James gave her a quick

one-armed hug. "The answer is yes." He poured himself a cup of coffee. "Where's Wonder Boy?"

"Look out the window."

"Ha! A fort! I remember building one like that as a boy. Is it okay with you that he's creating havoc in your yard?"

"Of course. He's having fun."

"Where's Sebastian?" asked James.

"Right here." Sebastian came into the kitchen, fully dressed. "Hi, James. Hey, Kabey." He used his old pet name for his daughter.

Kennedy lifted a beaming face to her father. "Hi, Daddy."

"How do you feel?"

"Like a wheelbarrow full of potatoes," Kennedy told her father.

"You don't look it," Sebastian lied, sitting down next to her.

Nicole placed the plate of eggs and bacon in front of Kennedy.

Kennedy stared ruefully down at the food. "Mommy always used to serve such *healthy* meals," she said mournfully. "Fruit for breakfast, with granola and raisins and dried cranberries."

Nicole stood very still. Her mind raced. Why was Kennedy so obviously setting her up? Kennedy had asked for bacon and eggs, and now that she had them, she wanted fruit and granola? Food was not the issue here, clearly. Nicole would not rise to the bait.

Forcing a smile, Nicole asked, "Kennedy, would you prefer fruit and granola? We have both."

"I don't want to be any trouble," Kennedy pouted.

"No trouble at all," Nicole purred. Reaching out, she moved the plate of bacon and eggs from Kennedy's spot to James's. "Here, James, why don't you have these?"

"Great, thanks." James picked up his knife and fork.

Smoothly but quickly, like Martha Stewart on ice skates, Nicole took out a bowl, a box of granola, and a spoon. She set them before Kennedy. She poured skim milk into a pitcher and set it next to the bowl.

Plucking a banana from the fruit bowl in the middle of the table, Nicole extended it to Kennedy. "Would you like to slice this onto your granola?" *Round one to me*, Nicole thought.

Kennedy nearly quivered with stifled indignation. Her eyes slid over to her husband, happily stuffing the rich creamy eggs into his mouth.

"Oh," Kennedy bleated, pressing her belly. "I feel so awful."

"Maybe you should go lie down," Sebastian suggested.

"Try to eat a little," Nicole urged in honeyed tones. "Your blood sugar is low in the morning."

With a heavy sigh, Kennedy poured the milk, sliced the banana, and ate the granola.

"Feel better?" Nicole inquired sweetly.

Kennedy ignored her. "Daddy, would you take me shopping like you did when I was young?"

"Sure, honey, but I don't think there are any maternity shops on the island."

"I don't need maternity clothes, silly daddy," Kennedy laughed. "I'm thinking some nice winter boots, maybe a purse . . . and I can always use jewelry, of course."

"Kennedy, you little minx," James teased, "why don't you wait and see what you get for Christmas?"

"Because I want to be with my daddy," Kennedy cooed.

"Get some clothes on, princess," Sebastian said. "I'll take you wherever you want to go."

Kennedy threw her arms around Sebastian. "Oh, thank you, Daddy. And will you take me out to lunch, too? Just you and me?"

Sebastian gave his winsome daughter a doting glance. "Of course. Where do you want to eat?"

"Oh, I don't care," Kennedy told him. "Any place where the food is hot and plentiful." Clumsily, she rose from her chair and shuffled into her bedroom to dress.

In a low voice, Sebastian asked James, "Do you mind that I'm going off for a private lunch with Kennedy?"

"Are you kidding? This will give me a chance to spend some time alone with Maddox. Besides," James winked, "I'm kind of *persona non grata* with Kennedy right now."

"You are? Why?"

"Because she's pregnant and I'm not."

The two men shared a conspiratorial chuckle.

Nicole busied herself at the sink, forcing back a gulp of self-pity. Everyone in the house had intimate knowledge of pregnancy and birth. James had, and was sharing it with Kennedy. Sebastian had shared it with Katya. Nicole had never been pregnant. As a nurse, she'd seen babies come into the world, but she'd never had her own.

"Thanks, Nicole." James brought his empty plate and silverware to the sink. "That was a treat."

His friendliness flashed over her like warmth. He headed through the mudroom to the back door. "Maddox!" he called. "Hey, Mad Man! Guess what?"

Nicole watched out the window as James squatted down to peer inside the fort. A moment later, Sebastian's arms circled her waist. His breath stirred her hair.

"You don't mind, do you?" he whispered. "I think Kennedy will be more receptive to you once she sees you haven't come between us."

"Of course I don't mind," Nicole lied. She wanted to burst into tears. She wanted to stamp her food like a child, crying, *Everyone's leaving me out!* Turning in his arms, she snuggled against him, soaking in the steadiness of his love.

"Daddy, I'm ready!" Kennedy entered the kitchen, chic in her camel-hair coat and tasseled wool hat.

"I'll get my coat," Sebastian said, going into the front hall.

"I'll go out back and tell Maddox and James goodbye," Kennedy said. "Meet you outside."

Kennedy walked right past Nicole and out the door without saying a word, as if Nicole didn't even exist.

13

❄

Kennedy linked her arm through her father's as they strolled down India Street toward town. Her heart swelled with triumph. A light snow was just beginning to fall, its flakes as white and soft as down, making the day even more magical.

"I love being here with you, Daddy." She leaned her head against his arm for a moment.

"I'm glad, Kabey."

"Let's look at the windows on Main Street," Kennedy suggested. "The merchants are always so clever." She was subtly steering her father toward lower Main Street and the Jewel of the Isle. Truly, she deserved a diamond for Christmas, and she knew she wasn't getting one from James because she'd had a secret shuffle through his desk and discovered he was giving her a new Mercedes SUV. Nice, but of course he was being more practical than romantic. He wanted his precious children to ride in safety.

"Oh." Kennedy gripped her father's arm. "Stop a minute."

Concerned, Sebastian inquired, "Are you having a contraction?"

"Yes. Don't worry. They're just Braxton Hicks. I went into the hospital three times with Maddox, thinking I was starting labor."

The Nantucket Pharmacy had an ice-skating scene in the window. Fluffy white fleece surrounded a pond made from an oval mirror. Elves, Santa, and a couple of reindeer pirouetted over the shimmering "ice." Snow people made of cotton balls with candy eyes, noses, and mouths stood next to Christmas trees adorned with tiny blinking lights. Mrs. Santa bent over an open box of chocolates, as if deciding which to choose first.

"Cute," Sebastian said.

"Adorable. Lucky Mrs. Santa. She can eat all the chocolate she wants."

"Why can't you?" her father asked.

"Daddy! I'm already a whale." Kennedy tugged on his arm. "I'm okay now. Let's walk some more."

A fabulous Icelandic sweater in the window of Peach Tree's caught her eye, but she bypassed it, determined to get her diamond.

"Shall we walk down to Straight Wharf and buy a few

wooden toys for Maddox at the Toy Boat?" Sebastian suggested.

Her father was heading them in the perfect direction. She squeezed his arm. "Good idea."

In the small fisherman's cottage housing the Toy Boat, Sebastian strode around gleefully, seeming like a kid himself. "Lighthouses, ferries, sailboats—so much to choose from. What do you think, Kennedy?"

Kennedy started to warn her father not to spoil Maddox, but bit her tongue. What she thought was that she wanted her father to spoil *her*. Why did children get all the goodies? The mommies did all the work. Sure, James had Maddox today, but most days of the year, her husband escaped their chaotic house wearing suit and tie, heading to the sophisticated adult world while Kennedy wrestled Maddox into the car for preschool then returned to the grocery shopping, laundry, and dishes.

She could understand now why her mother had employed a live-in nanny. Kennedy did have several good babysitters, and a cleaning service that came in twice a week. The laundry did James's shirts. They ate out or brought in takeout several times a week, especially since this second pregnancy. Compared to many others, she was spoiled, but she certainly didn't *feel* spoiled.

Kennedy loved Maddox with all her heart. He was the

light of her life. But nothing had prepared her for the noise, the mess, the constant, relentless neediness of a child.

Thank goodness Maddox enjoyed the preschool he attended in the morning. In the afternoon she tried to coax him into napping, but he was a living typhoon. In a month, she'd be saddled with two children, a baby who wouldn't sleep at night and a boy who tore around all day.

And yet . . . something deep within her cherished all this. Kennedy admired her mother intensely and wanted to be just like her, except perhaps a bit less perfect, which heaven knew was easy to achieve. Kennedy remembered the messes—real and emotional—she'd made as a child and how her nanny had consoled her and helped Kennedy clean them up. There'd been something so warm, so real, so *bonding* about those times. She wanted to provide that for her own children, even if she did it imperfectly, and oh boy, did she do it imperfectly.

If only someone would understand. No one ever praised mothers for the tedious work of child caring. No one ever gave a mother an award for not losing her temper ten times a day or for cajoling a kid to eat his vegetables. James tried to sympathize, but he was preoccupied with his work.

Perhaps that was why Kennedy wanted her father to give her something, a spontaneous surprise to show her that *she* was the light of *his* life. Something like—a diamond?

Returning along Main Street, they passed Jewel of the Isle.

"Oh," Kennedy gasped. "Isn't that pretty!"

Sebastian paused, grateful for an opportunity to set the bags full of toys down and relax his hands. "What, sweetheart?"

"That diamond Christmas tree brooch. So sweet."

Sebastian peered in the window. "It's nice." Suddenly an idea struck him. "Let's go in, Kennedy."

Inside, the shop sparkled with gemstones, silver, and gold. Kelli Trainor approached them. "Hello, Mr. Somerset. Merry Christmas."

"Merry Christmas, Kelli. Could you tell me, how much is that Christmas tree brooch in the window?"

Kellie lifted the pin out and set it, in its black velvet box, on the glass counter. She named a price.

Sebastian asked Kennedy, "I think that's reasonable, don't you? The diamonds are quite clear."

"It's gorgeous, Daddy," Kennedy gushed. She was almost fainting. It was a Christmas fairy tale. Her father had sensed her wish without a word, almost as if they had ESP!

"I'll take it." Sebastian removed his wallet from his pocket and slid out a credit card.

"Would you like that wrapped?" Kelli asked.

Kennedy opened her mouth to suggest they pin it on her coat instead, but before she could speak, her father nodded.

"Yes, please, Kelli." He beamed when he looked over at Kennedy. "Thanks for suggesting it, Kennedy. Nicole will be so surprised. I never think to buy her romantic presents. She's been working so hard trying to make this a perfect holiday for everyone. I can't wait to see her face when she opens the package on Christmas morning."

Kennedy's mouth fell open. Her throat closed tight with dismay.

"That's so sweet," Kelli said, filling the awkward silence.

"Next—" Sebastian's chest swelled with satisfaction as he tucked the wrapped package in with the others.

"Yes, Daddy?" Kennedy widened her eyes innocently.

"Where shall we have lunch? Someplace cozy. The wind's whipping the snow around."

Kennedy trudged next to her father in silence as they headed to the Brotherhood of Thieves. She was blind to the holiday-bright windows. Her father hummed "White Christmas," totally unaware of the disappointment steaming off her. She wanted to stop right there on the brick sidewalk next to the damned Christmas tree, throw her head back, and bawl. Everything was wrong. This holiday sucked. She was a warthog of a woman with a belly that weighed down her every move. She couldn't look sexy for her husband, she couldn't even look pretty, and when she tried to look winsome for her own father, what did he do? He bought diamonds not for his own daughter who was carrying his second grandchild, but for his new wife, who wouldn't even care about them. Who certainly wouldn't know how to wear them! Nicole was so more a rhinestone person, she didn't have the elegance to appreciate diamonds. What a waste. While Kennedy, at a time in her life when she could use some affection and pampering and *gratitude* didn't even get a stupid silver bracelet!

Did Nicole have some kind of psychological hold over her father? Did Nicole plant drugs in his coffee? She was way less attractive than Katya, she had no sense of style, she was like a cleaning woman who got to sit with the family, and Sebastian had bought her diamonds? Kennedy wanted to shriek.

"Here we are." Sebastian ushered his daughter into the brick-walled bistro. "After we eat, maybe you'll have the energy to look at boots."

"Boots," Kennedy muttered.

The hostess appeared and seated them in the front room next to the heartening warmth of the fireplace.

They removed their coats, settled in, and ordered. Sebastian remarked, "You seem upset."

Kennedy bit her lower lip. "I guess . . . I didn't realize you were so . . . enamored of Nicole."

Her father threw back his head and laughed. "Honey, Nicole is my wife. I would certainly hope I'd be enamored of her." He gave Kennedy a concentrated gaze. "But you're not pleased about this?"

She lowered her eyes and played with her napkin, folding it in different shapes as she talked. "I want you and Mom to get back together."

"Oh, Kabey, that's not going to happen. Be realistic, Kennedy. Your mother left me for Alonzo—"

"But they're not married!" Kennedy protested.

Sebastian shrugged. "Katya probably won't marry again. Your mother likes to have things her own way. As you are now aware, marriage is full of compromises. Come on, Kennedy, you've seen Katya. She's completely fine without me. She's got her own apartment where Alonzo can visit, but it's her place, and she doesn't want it messed up. She's almost sixty, after all. She deserves to spoil herself for a while. So do I, for that matter. I worked hard, providing for my family. Your mother worked hard, raising you and keeping house. Now we want to enjoy life, be free, even a bit silly, before we end up in our rocking chairs."

Kennedy gripped her father's hand. "Daddy, you're not *old*!"

"I'm not young, either. I'm healthy. And now, thanks to Nicole, I'm happy. That's a lot."

Kennedy wanted to appeal prettily, "Don't *I* make you happy?" but at that moment the waiter arrived with their meals.

"It means the world to me that James is such a nice man," Sebastian said as he picked up his fork. "He loves you and Maddox. That's obvious. That's the best gift any father can have, a good, trustworthy, loving son-in-law."

Kennedy conceded reluctantly, "Yes. James's great."

"I wish you could learn to like Nicole," Sebastian continued. "She's a wonderful person, and she would love to be part of your life."

"But she's not my mom," Kennedy reminded him.

"True. Nicole is completely different from Katya. She's not as concerned about style, she's a bit more into politics, she's a nurse, and she likes being part of the community. You know your mother, Kennedy. Katya always wanted to be seen as being *above* the community. Better than."

This was true, but Kennedy protested, "Please don't say negative things about my mother. It hurts my feelings."

"I'm sorry, Kennedy. Let's change the subject. What did you get James for Christmas?"

"Just some outdoor gear ordered from catalogs," she replied. "After all, I'm about to give him another son."

"I'm glad you brought that up. I feel kind of lousy, joining your mother and James at the hospital and leaving out Nicole."

This conversation was SO not going the way she'd planned! "She can hang out in the waiting room with Alonzo," Kennedy suggested.

Sebastian patted her hand. "I think you need a nap."

Kennedy wanted to say she needed a diamond brooch, but she kept her silence and focused on her food. If only she weren't so tired with this pregnancy, she'd have better ideas about how to get her parents back together, or at least how to get rid of Nicole. But her father was right. She was tired. She'd think more clearly after a nap.

Because she wasn't finished yet.

Whatever happened, Kennedy suddenly wondered, to Cinderella's father and the wicked stepmother after Cinderella married the prince?

14

❄

The snow was coming down quickly now, coating the lawn with a layer of pristine white. Snix was cold, and he was hungry.

He was also curious. This morning he'd hidden in a hedge to watch a boy build a peculiar house, a kind of cave, perfectly dog-sized. His father had come out to help him reinforce it with layers from cardboard boxes, covered with some old blankets, then wrapped around and around the outside with duct tape.

Now the boy and his father had gone. It seemed all the humans had gone.

Snix trotted to the funny makeshift house. Easing his way between two lawn chairs tilted on their sides, he entered.

It was warm. Cushions covered the floor. No snow got in. It would be the best place to sleep at night!

But as hard as he sniffed, he could find no food in here.

Reluctantly, he left the warm cave for the cold snowy outer world. Time for another food quest. Before he ventured away, he peed on a bush, the side of the garage, and the side of the house, so he'd be sure to know where to return.

He headed toward town. Many of the narrower streets were still and empty, the owners of the houses away in their winter homes, the windows dark, the trash barrels scentless. He found his way to Centre Street, where the aroma of bacon drifted from the Jared Coffin House like a love song, but the trash barrels had special locks on them, probably against marauding cats.

Across the street, Le Lanquedoc was shut tight. He trotted past the brick town buildings and the Whaling Museum until he came to the most likely place to find food.

Broad Street. Steamboat Wharf. Dog heaven. Taco Taco. Walters gourmet sandwiches to go. A pizza place. A coffee shop. The trash barrels lids were not so tightly fit, and being this close to the water, the ravaging gulls often did the work of breaking and entering for Snix.

Sure enough, in an alley he found a barrel on its side, papers and cups spilling out. A group of sky rats were pecking away at the contents.

He hesitated. Gulls were mean. They were almost bigger than Snix. Those beaks were as sharp as knives. His only hope was to fake it, so he charged toward them, barking savagely, showing his white pointed teeth. To his relief, with much irate screeching, the birds flew away.

He'd gotten there in time. Nosing away the papers, he hunted out buns, taco shells, hamburger, and cold fries. His belly swelled. He felt so much better. So much stronger. So much more hopeful.

He ate until he couldn't squeeze another morsel into his body. Replete, his body begged for sleep.

He retraced his steps to the house with the warm cave. People were out on the streets, calling out gleefully about the snow, elated that it was going to be a white Christmas. Snix wasn't so pleased. He was scared. Still, it swelled his heart to see so many people smiling, chatting, waving, dressed in red, white, and green, their arms full of packages. It made the world seem like a friendlier place.

Near Nantucket Bookworks, a teenage boy noticed Snix. "Hi, guy," the kid said, reaching down to scratch Snix between the ears. "Aren't you a cute little pooch."

Snix cocked his head, trying to send a message: *Take me home with you*.

A girl came out of the shop, a book bag in her hand. "Okay," she said, "now let's go to Murray's Toggery. I'll get Dad a sweater." She linked her arm through the boy's and led him away, not even aware of Snix sitting there wagging his tail. The boy walked off.

But the friendly warmth of his touch remained, all through Snix's body.

He continued on his way, back through the maze of narrow lanes, until he found his own scent on a bush. The house had lights on inside, but he heard no sounds of people, so he took a chance and dashed straight into the backyard and through the lawn chairs into the cave.

Oh, it was warm. The cushions were soft. The wind howled but no snow made its way inside. His belly was full. His neck had been scratched. A human had told him he was cute. Curling up in comfort, Snix fell asleep.

15

❄

After breakfast, Nicole cleaned the kitchen. Upstairs, she made all the beds. She considered picking up the clothes littering her stepdaughter-in-law's floor and putting them in the laundry basket, because it had to be difficult for Kennedy to bend over. On the other hand, Princess Kennedy might object to Nicole touching her things, so she let them lie. She did a quick run through the house with the vacuum.

As she worked, she longed to wallow in the delicious self-indulgent behavior she once treated herself with as a widow. She could no longer curl up on the sofa shoveling popcorn into her mouth while watching *Terms of Endearment* and weeping so hard she choked on her popcorn. Sebastian was too elegant to imagine she could behave in such a churlish manner, so she restrained herself. Frankly, she missed it.

She phoned Jilly. "I'm a pariah in my own house."

"Poor thing. Come to Mama."

"I've got too much to do."

"Nonsense. If they can go out to lunch, so can we. It's snowing, Nicole. Look out the window! We can take a long walk on the beach and let the wind blow away our troubles, then have clam chowder at Met on Main."

Nicole hesitated.

"Oh, you'd rather stay home and sulk?" Jilly teased.

"I'll meet you at the Hub in ten minutes."

Putting on her snow boots immediately lifted Nicole's mood. Brown suede with thick rubbery soles, they were lined with white fleece and had red and green tartan laces. She pulled on her puffy red down coat and a red wool hat adorned with a knit green holly leaf, complete with red berry, shouldered her purse, slid on her red mittens and hurried out into the invigorating air.

Jilly was already at the Hub, festive in green wool coat and hand-knit creamy white cap and muffler. She greeted Nicole with a big hug and kiss. "Let's walk down to Straight Wharf and then over to the town beach."

"Good idea." Nicole glanced around. "People are out shopping."

"I've done all mine. I've got two duffel bags full of presents to take to Boston when we go for Christmas with the grandchildren."

"You leave tomorrow?" They passed Peach Tree's. "Great sweater."

"I know. Don't tempt me." They walked on toward the water. "First thing."

"I'll miss you," Nicole said.

"You'll be fine. Christmas is in two days. They leave on the twenty-seventh. You can survive that long."

Buoyed by her friend's companionship, Nicole thought just maybe she could. "Maddox is an adorable child, and James is nice. He tries hard to be pleasant to everyone. But I swear Kennedy is on some kind of campaign to make me lose my cool. She's absolutely devious, Jilly." As they ambled along through the falling snow, Nicole described the morning's breakfast psychodrama with the bacon and eggs.

"You're attributing too much premeditation to her," Jilly insisted. "Kennedy's a nice enough girl, as I recall. She's pregnant, remember? Pregnancy makes you irrational. Give her a break."

"You're right," Nicole conceded reluctantly. "I just wish Sebastian would stick up for me more. He always seems to think his daughter is flawless."

"Typical father," Jilly said knowingly. "I can't tell you the times Bob and I have argued over something Stacey's done or wants to do. He always takes her side. I'm always the disciplinarian. But in a few days, Kennedy will go home and you'll have Seb back for yourself."

Nicole's sigh of satisfaction was cut short. Across the street and down a block, she saw Sebastian and Kennedy leaving the Jewel of the Isle. Sebastian had a small dark green bag in his hand. He linked his arm through his daughter's and carefully escorted her around the corner onto Easy Street.

"Look." She nudged Jilly with her elbow. "Sebastian just bought Kennedy some jewelry."

Jilly spotted the retreating pair. "It's Christmas, Nicole."

"Oh, I know! I hate the way I feel, like a sniveling jealous fairy-tale witch. Let's change the subject. Tell me what you're reading."

Both women were voracious readers. Books kept them talking for the rest of their walk and most of their lunch at Fog Island. When they parted to go their separate ways, Nicole was back in her usual optimistic, level-headed mindset.

❄

In the early afternoon, Maddox and Kennedy took naps while the others lounged in bed or the den, reading and watching television. Kennedy was still sleeping when Maddox woke, so Nicole, who was in the kitchen, gave him permission to go in the backyard and build a snowman.

"I'm making pumpkin lasagna for tonight," she told the boy. "Just as soon as I put it in the oven, I'll come out and join you."

She helped him don his outdoor gear and watched as the child ran joyfully out into the snowy late afternoon. She sprinkled fresh Parmesan on the lasagna and slid it into the oven. As she rinsed and checked the fresh cranberries she would make for the duck sauce that evening, Sebastian came into the kitchen.

"Something smells appetizing."

"Good." Rinsing her hands, Nicole murmured, "I wish we had two ovens. I have to sort of stagger what I'm cooking with only one."

Sebastian snorted. "Sorry, Nicole. Cooking was never one of Katya's passions. One oven was more than enough for her."

Nicole bit her lip. She didn't enjoy hearing the words Katya and passion come out of her husband's mouth.

As if he'd guessed her thoughts, Sebastian drew Nicole into his arms. "I hope you realize how grateful I am for all you're doing. Not just the decorating and the cooking, but making the house feel so warm. You've got a gift for perking up people, Nicole."

For half a second, Nicole considered pointing out that

she certainly didn't please Kennedy. But that would have been churlish, especially with her husband's arms around her. "I hope I perk you up, Sebastian."

"Let's go upstairs and I'll show you," Sebastian murmured into her neck.

Nicole drew away in pretend horror. "In the daytime? With your family here?" Secretly, she was tickled.

James chose that moment to come into the kitchen from the birthing room. "Time for a drink yet?" he asked. "Kennedy's sound asleep."

"Maddox is out trying to build a snowman," Nicole told him. "I promised I'd go help him, but I got delayed with cooking and um, everything."

James looked out the window. "Is Mad in the backyard or the front?"

"The backyard, of course." Nicole checked her watch. With a playful glance at Sebastian, she said, "Dinner's ready in about an hour."

"I'll play with him until then." James went out the door.

"Alone at last," Nicole's husband said, pulling her close once more.

16

❄

Maddox stood in the backyard with his tongue protruding, trying to catch the flakes of snow that the wind flung into his eyes and up his nose. When his tongue got cold, he decided to go into his fort.

Snow had settled on top of his hideaway. On one side, snow drifted up into a wall. Maddox dropped to his knees and crawled between the lawn chairs into the warm security of his cave.

It was dark inside. He blinked, thinking about this, trying to understand. Back in the real world, the sun had almost set, but some pale rays still illuminated the sky and the brightness of the snow reflected back the shine. In here—with cardboard walls secured by duct tape wrappings and a ceiling of picnic table wood—no snow entered, and not much light.

After a moment, his eyes adjusted to the dim interior. It was nice and warm compared to the chill outside. Maddox crawled farther in and closed the cardboard flap that served as a door. Now it was supercozy.

Except . . .

Something was in the corner. Something as big as Maddox. Something dark, at least it looked dark, and as Maddox watched, it moved.

Too paralyzed with terror even to squeak, Maddox stared at the lump. A wolf? No, wolves were bigger. A rat? No, rats were smaller. A rabbit? That would be okay, but it wasn't rabbit shaped.

An eye gleamed through the darkness.

Maddox didn't know what to do. Should he pretend to be something not alive, a big rock, for example? Should he try to be friendly? How fast could he exit the cave before whatever it was leapt at him, catching him by his shoe?

The creature stirred. Two eyes shone. It appeared to be in no hurry to eat Maddox. He knew it wasn't a lion or a bear; Daddy said those didn't exist on the island. Perhaps it was a baby deer? But the thing shuffled into a standing position, and its legs were not nearly long enough to be a deer's. Was it a cat?

"Hello?" Maddox whispered. "Kitty kitty?"

Encouraged by his voice, the animal slowly, cautiously, moved toward Maddox, stumbling slightly on the uneven cushions, until Maddox could see that the creature was a furry brown dog with black button eyes like his toy animals and a pink tongue peeking between small white teeth.

"Hi, guy." Maddox held out his hand the way his mommy had taught him, so the dog could sniff him, so the dog wouldn't feel threatened.

The dog sniffed Maddox. Its dark eyes raised expectantly to meet Maddox's eyes, and its tail wagged hopefully.

"Who are you?" Maddox asked. "Are you lost?"

The dog dropped to its belly and crept closer to Maddox, still wagging its tail. Maddox reached out and patted the dog's head. The dog responded by scooting even nearer, keeping his yearning black eyes on Maddox's face.

"You're a nice doggy, aren't you?" Maddox said. "What's your name? Where's your collar?" He felt around the dog's neck but no leather or metal met his fingers.

The dog, encouraged by the touching, moved closer to Maddox and licked his fingers.

A wonderful thought suddenly appeared in Maddox's mind. Could Santa have brought him this dog for Christmas?

But Christmas wasn't for two more days. And his mom didn't want a dog.

Running his fingers over the animal, he felt its ribs. Even as a small boy, he understood that the dog hadn't had much to eat recently. This dog was lost. And hungry. Maybe this dog was hiding from a mean owner. Maddox had once seen a man kick a dog. Maybe this dog had run away. Maddox knew what it felt like to want to run away.

"Maddox!" His father's voice boomed out into the yard, making Maddox jump with surprise.

"Just a minute, boy," Maddox whispered. He crawled out the lawn chair entrance, stuck his head up, and called, "I'm here, Daddy, in my fort."

"Let's build a snowman. We've got time before dinner."

"Okay, Daddy. I'll be right there."

Back in the fort, the dog sat very obediently, his eyes searching Maddox's face.

"You're hungry," Maddox whispered, "but I can't bring you into the house because Mommy wouldn't like that. I'll sneak food out after dinner, I promise. Lots of good food, okay?"

The dog wagged his tail.

Delight flashed through Maddox as he realized he had a secret friend, his own private buddy. He could have adventures with this dog!

The dog needed a name. Maddox thought of famous best friends. Frog and Toad. Well, he couldn't call a dog Frog or Toad, that would be silly. He giggled to himself and the dog caught his mood, wiggling all over and climbing into Maddox's arms, licking his chin, wagging his tail. Christopher Robin and Winnie the Pooh! Maddox fell over backward, snickering.

"Pooh!" he gurgled as the dog licked his face. "I'll name you Pooh." Pooh was one of Maddox's favorite words because it had two meanings, one that could make his grandmother Katya raise her eyebrows. He hugged Pooh, who was cuddling as close as he could get.

"Maddox?" His father's voice sounded again.

"Coming!" Maddox answered. He sat up and put his hands on the dog's face. "Now listen. I have to go in. You stay here. I'll bring you some food as soon as I can, okay? You'll be nice and warm here. I'll be back pretty soon."

Pooh cocked his head, his dark eyes deep with intelligence, as if he understood every word.

❄

Daddy decided they should build the snowman in the front yard so people could see him. He showed Maddox how to squeeze the snow tight to pack it. Together they rolled up three balls, stacking them up before adding fallen sticks for arms. Daddy opened the front door, calling in to ask Nicole for a carrot for the nose while Maddox looked beneath the bushes until he found two rocks for the eyes. The rocks were different sizes, so the snowman looked kind of funny but still cute.

When they stepped inside, the house seemed hot and bright. As his father helped him strip off his snow boots, mittens, coat, and hat, Maddox realized how dark it looked outside if you were inside a building, even though a pearly sheen of light lingered in the air from streetlights and moonlight falling on the snow.

"Let's wash your hands and face," Daddy said, taking Maddox's hand and leading him to the bathroom.

Mommy was up, sitting in the living room talking to Granddad. Nicole was trotting back and forth between the kitchen and the dining room. Maddox loved washing his hands and playing with the water. He could make lines of water run one way or the other and splash pools in the sink.

"Enough," his father said. "You're getting your sweater wet. Come on, Maddox."

Reluctantly, Maddox slowly turned off the faucets and dried his hands. Here came the boring part of his day, sitting at the dining room table with adults. They took so long to eat their food! He could gobble his down and be ready to play in a jiffy, but his parents wanted him to sit there like a statue, not rocking back and forth on his chair or tapping his fingers on the table or swinging his feet or even making fart noises with his mouth. This was one of the many things he couldn't understand about adults.

The food smelled good, though. His mommy insisted he eat some of the yucky lettuce salad, and he forced himself to swallow a few bites of the cranberry sauce, but the dark meat on his plate that his mommy said was duck made him cringe. Maddox preferred meat in tiny ground pieces, not hunks. Fortunately, the pumpkin lasagna had lots of creamy cheese, so he had two helpings of it, and all the adults praised him.

He had an awesome thought. Pooh would like the duck! He had to think of a way to smuggle it to the dog. He considered various options while the adults blabbed away, their cheeks growing rosy as they ate the warm food and drank their wine. The table was pretty with glowing candles making the silver shine. It was nice, seeing his parents having a good time with Granddad and Nicole. When Granddad got up to pour Daddy more wine, he blocked Maddox from his mother's vision for a few seconds, just enough time for Maddox to sneak a chunk of duck into his trouser pocket. Then he got the cool idea of putting the meat in his mouth, pretending to chew, then wiping his mouth with his napkin and spitting the meat into the napkin. Pretty soon he had a nice glob of meat to take to Pooh.

Maddox was proud. This must be how it felt to be a superhero.

17

❄

After dinner, everyone but Kennedy helped Nicole carry the plates, glasses, and platters into the kitchen. Even Maddox willingly skipped back and forth with his utensils and napkin. Kennedy sat at the table, grounded like a blimp, listening to all the others chatter as they loaded the dishwasher and put away leftovers. How peppy they sounded. She put her elbows on the table and dropped her head in her hands.

She heard James yell, "Maddox, where are you going?"

Maddox called back, "I left something in my fort."

The back door slammed.

"You need a coat!" James cautioned, noting in a lower voice, "That kid. Where does he get his energy?" James flicked on the back outdoor light.

The back door slammed again as Maddox returned.

"Don't go out again without a coat," his father ordered

him. "And stamp your feet on the mudroom rug. Don't track snow through the house."

Kennedy's father clapped his hands in the front hall. "Okay, everyone. Time to see Christmasland!"

"What's that, Granddad?"

"You'll see. Put on your coat. We won't be leaving the car, so you don't have to bundle up too much." Sebastian came into the dining room. "You're coming with us, aren't you, Kabey?" Lowering his voice, he added enticingly, "Over by Surfside Road, it looks like the North Pole. Several of the streets have houses with every kind of lighted holiday spectacle you can imagine. Santa and his reindeer and sleigh on the roof. Frosty the Snowman. Beautiful life-size crèches."

Kennedy placed her hands on her belly. "I'd love to go but I'm not feeling very good. I'm not sure the food agreed with me. Duck is so rich."

"Would you like some bicarb of soda in water?"

"That would be great, Daddy, thanks."

Her father went off to the kitchen. Kennedy hauled herself up from the table and slowly lumbered into the living room, where she collapsed on a sofa.

"Mommy, aren't you coming?" Maddox asked.

"Not tonight, sweetie." Kennedy smoothed her son's ruffled hair. "You go with Daddy and Granddad."

"Nicole, too." Maddox's eyes were shining with excitement, his cheeks rosy from his run out into the cold.

"My big boy." Kennedy hugged him to her as well as she could. "I love you, Mad Man."

The others congregated in the front hall, pulling on gloves and coats while Nicole did her St. Martyr of the Household bit again, bringing Kennedy a pile of magazines and tucking a blanket over her feet. Maddox was jumping up and down with anticipation. Kennedy's father helped Nicole into her down coat. Kennedy felt childishly miffed at herself. Everyone else was giddy and good-natured. She was like a fat female Scrooge.

As soon as she saw the Grand Cherokee's lights fade into the distance, she levered herself off the sofa. Trundling up the stairs to the second floor, she headed down the long hall to the last small room, used as a storage room. Turning on the light, she was pleased to see that nothing had changed. Her grandmother's wedding gown was still zipped in a dress bag, hanging from the back of the closet. Her ice skates, skis, and rollerblades were in the closet, along with a few of her more memorable Halloween costumes and her father's high school letter jacket. One wall was lined with shelves filled with books. Her favorite books from childhood had been pillaged to take to her home to read to Maddox. Her high school and college yearbooks were still here.

The family photo albums were here, too. Ha.

Kennedy had been a child before digital cameras hit the scene, so her parents had devotedly snapped shots, had them printed off, and slipped the best photos into handsome leather-bound albums. Getting to them now was difficult, because they lined the lowest shelves, requiring Kennedy to squat—not her easiest posture—to wrench them out of the tightly packed shelf. They were heavy, fat, and bulky. Still, she persevered, tugging them off the shelf until she had them in a pile. Then, two by two, she carried them downstairs to the living room coffee table. It was a time-consuming process. She could heft only two at a time, and she had to hold those against her body with one arm so she could grasp the stair banister with her free hand. Fourteen unwieldy albums, compressing so many years of her family's life. Huffing, puffing, gasping, wheezing, Kennedy climbed down and back up, down and back up, her lower back cramping with protest at the weight.

Finally they were gathered on the coffee table. Excellent. Nicole's prissy Christmas room with its tree, stockings, and small wooden crèche was overwhelmed by the stack of albums. Kennedy dropped like a stone onto the sofa and caught her breath. Her back was a red hot coal of tongs squeezing her spinal cord, but she wasn't ready to rest yet. She spread as many of the albums as she could, open, photos gleaming, on the coffee table. The others she stacked on the floor in small towers of memory.

After resting, she scanned the albums until she found the one filled with pictures of herself at three, chubby and grinning from her father's arms, her mother next to them. Oh, she had been such a darling baby. Her three-year-old self sat smiling on Christmas morning, holding a baby doll in her arms. Katya wore a red and green silk robe; she was astonishingly lovely as she sat on the sofa with Sebastian's arm wrapped around her, both of them flushed with pleasure. Kennedy left that album open on the table so Nicole wouldn't fail to notice it.

Leaning back against the sofa, Kennedy allowed herself a great big helping of self-pity. Why did everything change?

A few photos of her nanny, Patty, had been included in the album. Kennedy happily remembered the woman, who smelled of sugar, flour, and baby powder. Here Kennedy was, taking her first brave steps toward Patty. Here Kennedy was with Patty at the ocean. The reality of being so young floated just out of the grasp of Kennedy's memory, but as she opened more albums, she began to warp back into some of the scenes.

The Halloween when she was four, dressed as a princess. She'd never wanted to take those sparkling clothes off. In fact, she recalled having a fight about it with Patty because she wanted to wear the princess gown and tiara to school.

The Christmas she was ten, memorable because Patty had been let go because Kennedy was considered too old to need a nanny. The family had gone to Aruba for Christmas. Such shimmering turquoise blue water, the palm trees, the cottage that had no television set.

Changing years, changing holiday islands. Rain forests, thatched cottages without walls, hotel rooms with television sets, her mother lying on a beach lounge, eyes covered with sunglasses, turning deep brown in the sun, then dressing for dinner and dancing with Sebastian and their friends. Kennedy got to order room service and watch videos.

Katya's clothes. Swirling silks, a sleek black bikini, skin-sleek satin. Kennedy appreciated even more as an adult how beautiful Katya was and how hard she had worked in the service of that beauty. Not only the strict dieting and exercising, but the hours spent at the beauty salon, having her hair colored and styled, having her legs and eyebrows waxed—and Katya abhorred pain as much as Kennedy. All Kennedy's friends had Brazilian waxes, but Kennedy couldn't bring herself to do it. She could hardly bear to have her legs waxed.

In all the photos, Katya's nails were perfectly shaped and painted. Discreet but expensive gems gleamed on her fingers and in her earlobes, around her neck and arms. Her mother had not been completely self-absorbed, though. She had taught Kennedy well, and Kennedy was grateful. Katya had shown Kennedy how to eat healthily if lightly, so that Kennedy didn't get caught up in the anorexia and bulimia of so many girls at her boarding school. That was a real victory.

Katya must have loved Sebastian passionately to have sacrificed the glory that was her body to the degradations of pregnancy and birth. How Katya had gotten her figure back after her pregnancy, Kennedy did not understand. She was sure she would resemble an exploded water balloon for the rest of her life.

"Mommy!" The front door burst open. Maddox ran into the room, forgetting in his excitement to be gentle with Kennedy, throwing himself onto her before even taking off his coat and mittens. "We saw Santa on his sleigh! We saw Rudolph! We saw Charlie Brown, and Snoopy on his doghouse! One house had lights ALL over!"

James stalked into the room. "Hey, kid, remember to be careful with Mommy and the baby."

Kennedy kissed Maddox's forehead. "Did Rudolph have a red nose?"

"He did, Mommy!"

Squirming slightly to shift her son's weight, Kennedy asked, "Was there a snowman?"

"Yeah! One house had a whole snow family!" In his excitement, he kneed Kennedy in the belly.

Kennedy couldn't help going "Oof!"

James noticed. Swinging his son up in his arms, he said, "Let's take your coat off, Maddox. It's time to calm down now and get ready for bed."

Kennedy sensed her husband's gaze resting on her, giving her a moment to offer to help put their son to bed, to ask about the outing, to send him a look of gratitude. She ignored him, staring intently at the album. She took care of Maddox ninety-nine percent of the time. It was James's turn. Besides, she had a scheme to put into action.

Sebastian and Nicole entered the living room, bringing a rush of fresh cold air with them. Kennedy shivered.

"How are you, Kabey?" her father asked.

"All right."

"Maybe tomorrow night you'll feel like driving over to see the lights," Nicole suggested. "They're amazing—"

Sebastian interrupted. "Kennedy, what's all this? Good Lord, you didn't haul all these albums down the stairs by yourself, did you?"

Elated by her father's concern, Kennedy ducked her head and peered up at her father from beneath her eyelashes. "I wanted to look at them. I wanted to remember all the wonderful times our family had during the holidays."

"But honey, you could have hurt yourself. You should have waited for us to come home and bring them down."

Nicole knelt by the coffee table, focusing on the album Kennedy had left open where Katya was at her most young and staggeringly gorgeous.

"Katya is such a true beauty," Nicole said, touching the photo with her forefinger. "But you know, Sebastian, I think your daughter is even more beautiful."

What? Kennedy wanted to totally *throw up*. Was Nicole demented? Was she some kind of frontal lobe victim? No, she was a genius at pretense, she wasn't going to let Kennedy get to her, she was acting like someone without a stick of jealousy, all gooiness.

"Nicole's right," Sebastian said. "You are more lovely than your mother, Kennedy."

Kennedy's lower lip trembled. "Thanks, Daddy." Bracing herself, she began the awkward effort of elevating her bulging body from the sofa. "I think I'll go to bed now. I did get tired, carrying all those albums. But they cheered me up, so it was worth it."

18

❄

Christmas Eve day, a storm was predicted by the Weather Channel, with rising winds toward evening, so after breakfast Nicole and Sebastian headed off to the grocery store. They needed to stock the house with perishables and last-minute goodies and pick up the fresh, twenty-one-pound turkey. Tonight Nicole was serving beef Wellington with lots of veggies and a pumpkin pie for dessert.

First Nicole and Sebastian dropped James and Maddox at the wharves to watch the ferries come home. The wind-driven current was so strong it slammed the great behemoth car ferry the *Eagle* into the side of the dock, crashing like thunder. Fishing boats were tied up to the piers, bobbing like bathtub toys in the churning harbor.

At Stop & Shop, Nicole and Sebastian loaded up the cart, lugging armfuls of bags out to the car.

"We bought fresh cream?" Nicole wondered aloud as they left the parking lot.

"We did. I checked it off the list. We're set," Sebastian assured her. "We have enough food to feed us for the next week."

"I hope so. If the storm is as bad as they say, the boats may not be able to make it over with fresh supplies for days."

Sebastian reached over and held her hand. "The storm might miss us and blow out to sea. If it does hit, we're in a house that's stood for over a hundred years. Twenty-five years ago, we had trouble with power going out, but the electric company installed an underwater cable, so we'll be just fine."

"Oh, heavens, I hadn't even thought about losing electricity."

"You worry too much," Sebastian said.

You don't have five people to feed three meals a day, Nicole wanted to remind him, but she didn't want to seem to be complaining. And she wasn't. She loved cooking. She loved the holiday season. She adored Maddox, liked James just fine . . . and she was proud of the way she was keeping her cool with Kennedy. She was unaccountably nervous, though, she was on edge, as if her women's intuition was warning her of trouble ahead. No doubt this was caused by the falling barometer, the increasing wind, and the frenzied ions or protons or whatever was invisibly frothing in the air.

They picked up a windblown James and Maddox and returned home. James helped Sebastian and Nicole carry in the multitude of bags.

Maddox ran straight to his mother. Kennedy was sitting in a chair by the fire in the living room.

"It was awesome, Mommy!" Maddox squealed, throwing himself into her lap.

"Ouch." Kennedy recoiled as her son literally knocked the breath out of her. Seeing Maddox's face flicker with anxiety, she reached out and pulled him up onto her knees, hugging him tightly. "I'm okay, sweetie. Now tell me all about the ocean. How high were the waves?"

"This high!" Maddox proudly raised his arm as far as it would go above his head.

"Wow." Kennedy widened her eyes in appreciative astonishment. "I hope you held Daddy's hand."

"I did, Mommy, I did. And the big ferry boat went *crash* into the—" He frowned, unsure of the right word.

"The dock?" Kennedy suggested, lovingly smoothing her son's hair.

"Yeah! And—" Maddox wiggled with excitement, describing the adventure.

Nicole hummed as she stripped off her coat and unpacked the groceries. It was good to see Kennedy happy. She put on Christmas music in her kitchen, and the sparkling arms of her holiday sweater brightened her mood as she worked. This was her favorite sweater, with Santa on his sleigh in the front, the reindeer prancing around the side so that Rudolph with his cherry-red nose glittered on her back.

She prepared an easy lunch of tomato soup and grilled cheese sandwiches (on whole wheat bread, of course).

Maddox was still overexcited from his outing, almost jumping up and down in his chair.

"Sit still, Maddox," Kennedy told her son. "You'll spill your soup." She looked tired. "James, would you help him with the soup? It's so difficult for a four-year-old to eat."

Nicole's heart cringed. "Tell you what." Quickly she rose from the table, easing Maddox's bowl away from him. "I'll pour your soup into a mug, and then you can drink it."

"Good idea," James affirmed.

Kennedy was silent as Nicole got down a Christmas mug.

"The snow's accumulating," Sebastian reported, turning the conversation to the view out the windows. "We don't usually have snow this soon," he explained to James. "Thirty miles out at sea, we're caught in the Gulf Stream, which keeps us warmer than the mainland."

"It's ideal for Christmas." Nicole set the mug in front of Maddox and resumed her seat. "It makes everything so pretty."

Kennedy rolled her eyes and sighed.

James, with an impatient thinning of his mouth, shot his wife a glance. "Are you okay, Kennedy?"

"As a matter of fact, no," Kennedy puffed. "I think I'm coming down with some kind of flu. Or something I ate last night didn't agree with me."

Sebastian leaned forward, concerned. "Perhaps you should go back to bed."

"It's Christmas Eve," Kennedy protested. "I don't want to lie in bed today."

Nicole took a deep breath. She kept her mouth shut. Let the men sort Kennedy out, she decided. Nothing Nicole could do or say would help.

"Want to read to Maddox by the fire?" Sebastian suggested.

"Good idea," James quickly agreed. "He's had a good outing this morning—"

James's words were interrupted by a loud pounding at the front door.

Nicole jumped up. "I'll get it. It might be presents from someone!" Hurrying optimistically down the hall, she threw open the front door, letting in a blast of cold air and snow.

A woman in a mink coat and hat strode past Nicole, slamming the door behind her, shaking flakes off her shoulders, stamping her leather high-heeled boots on the rug. She acted as if she were entering her own house.

Well, in a way, she was.

Nicole had never fainted but at this moment she had an excellent sense of how it might feel.

"Katya?" She had seen photos of Katya before, but she'd never laid eyes on the woman in person, in her glorious Technicolor glamour.

"Damn, it's wicked out there," Katya said. She stripped her leather gloves off her long hands and dropped them on the front hall table. "You've moved the front hall chair," she said to Nicole. "Where am I going to sit down to take off my boots?"

Nicole was speechless.

"Mommy?" Kennedy hurried into the hall, eyes wide. "Mommy! What are you doing here?"

"Oh, Kennedy." Katya turned her back on Nicole and held her arms out to her daughter. "Sweetie, thank heavens." She hugged Kennedy tightly.

Sebastian entered the hall, a perplexed expression on his face. "Katya?"

"Sebby." Reaching out, Katya put her hand on her ex-husband's chest. "I apologize for arriving like this, but I just *had* to be here with my family. Alonzo and I had a terrible fight." Katya's head drooped elegantly, like a tulip. "We're finished."

Kennedy's face lit up like a beacon. "You and Alonzo

broke up?" Her eyes fluttered back and forth between her father and mother.

Nicole allowed herself to tilt backward slightly, in order to be supported by the wall. She forced herself to breathe.

Sebastian stepped away from his ex-wife's touch. "Why did you come here?" he asked. His voice was cool, and for that Nicole was grateful.

Katya simpered. "I've spent practically every Christmas of my life in this house. Kennedy's here. My grandson is here. Where else could I turn for comfort?"

"You did the absolutely right thing, Mommy," Kennedy assured her mother.

Sebastian's face darkened. "Don't you think you're being rather insensitive?" he demanded.

Katya gazed innocently, widening her crystal-blue eyes. "What do you mean?"

Nicole's heart fluttered so rapidly she was afraid she was going to hyperventilate, pass out, and slide down the wall to the floor.

In three strides, Sebastian was next to Nicole. He put his arms around her shoulders. "This is Nicole's house now, not yours."

"Daddy!" Kennedy cried.

"Oh, surely—" Katya began to object.

"Grandmama!" Maddox ran into the hall and stared up at Katya, mouth open in wonder.

"Katya," James said, following his son. "What are you doing here?"

"James, darling. And precious Maddox, my own grandson." Katya knelt to embrace the boy. "Grandmama's here to spend Christmas with you, Maddox. Isn't that wonderful?"

19

❄

Her mother was here! Kennedy was breathless with amazement, and her heart seemed to be expanding alarmingly as emotions jostled within her.

Rapture at seeing her mother, actually here in this house.

Dismay at having her mother see her, Kennedy, who had allowed herself to relax. She hadn't put on her makeup yet, and it was already after lunch. She'd been lying down in front of the fire and hadn't brushed her hair since—well, she couldn't remember. Compared to Katya in her camel-hair trousers and cashmere sweater, her heavy gold necklace and earrings, Kennedy was absolutely frumpy in her red maternity tent.

Hope at the possibility of her parents getting back together, because here they both were in the same house, and Alonzo was in the past!

Despair at seeing her father move away from Katya to put his arm around Nicole.

"I need to sit down," she murmured.

"Of course you do, sweetheart." Katya handed her mink to James. Over her shoulder, she said to Sebastian, "My suitcase is on the front stoop. Could you bring it in, please?" With an arm around her daughter, she cooed, "Let's go into the living room and get you comfy."

They settled on the sofa. Kennedy angled her bulk to allow herself to study her mother's face. Katya's eyes were slightly pink and swollen. Obviously she had been crying, something she seldom allowed herself to do, and Kennedy's heart broke for her mother.

"Are you okay, Mommy?"

Katya bristled. "Don't I look okay?"

"Of course. You're as beautiful as always. But you must be sad without Alonzo."

Katya stared down at her hands. "Devastated." A shadow passed over her face.

In that moment, Kennedy saw the slight sag of flesh around her mother's lovely jawline and the pouch beneath her eyes that had not been quite disguised by concealer.

"Oh, Mommy."

Katya stiffened at the compassion in Kennedy's voice. "It happened only last night. I haven't slept. I know I look dreadful, but I'm extremely tired. Shattered, really, with the packing and the trip. It was a horrendous flight, very bumpy, the wind *shook* the plane. What I'd *adore* is a hot bath and a good nap."

"Of course," Kennedy began, just as her father walked into the room. Kennedy's spirits lifted. "Daddy, Mommy wants—"

"Katya." Sebastian's voice was terse. He remained standing. "You've got to realize how inappropriate it is for you to be here."

"Daddy!" Kennedy burst out.

"I'm sorry if you and Alonzo broke it off, but the fact is that is *your* matter to deal with, not mine. You and I were divorced years ago. You're a grown woman, you have plenty of financial resources—I've seen to that. You need to make other plans."

Katya slanted her head submissively. Fluttering her lashes, she pleaded, "I have no place else to go."

"You must have friends on the mainland," Sebastian pointed out.

Katya shrugged. "No one I could go to for the holiday."

"Fine. Then a hotel. You've always been fond of first-class hotels."

Kennedy's mood rose at this sign of her father remembering what her mother preferred.

"A hotel? On Christmas?"

"We've often stayed in hotels on Christmas," Sebastian reminded her as he stalked to the fire, stirred it with the poker, then shot Katya a sober stare. "I suggest you try to get a room at the Ritz or the Taj in Boston."

Katya lifted her shoulder coyly to her cheek. "I'm not sure I can leave the island. With this storm . . ."

Sebastian's face darkened with annoyance. Straightening, he decreed, "Then go to one of the hotels on Nantucket. The Jared Coffin House."

"The expense—" Katya started to object.

"I'll pay for it." Sebastian folded his arms over his chest, a sign that he was not going to yield.

Katya tossed her lovely blond hair. "Fine. But Sebastian, be kind. I'm so awfully tired. I was just telling Kennedy that I didn't sleep a wink last night. Couldn't I take a brief lie-down here before I go back out into the storm?"

"Please, Daddy," Kennedy begged. "Mommy can rest on my bed, and while she rests, I'll phone the Nantucket hotels and see who has a room."

Sebastian did not look pleased.

"Sebby." Katya stood up, stepping close to her ex-husband, putting her hand on his arm. "I'm sorry about all of this. I know I've made so many many terrible mistakes. If I could only turn back the clock . . ."

Kennedy watched her mother and father with hope springing up in her heart.

"You can't turn back time, Katya." Sebastian didn't sound angry or bitter or punitive, but adamant. Quietly, he walked away from her to the door into the front hall. "And I'm glad about that. Now please have some consideration and take yourself to a hotel."

Her father left the room.

Katya turned away so that Kennedy couldn't see her face. Kennedy's stomach cramped with regret and despair. It was not going to happen. Her parents were never going to get back together. That damned Nicole had bewitched her father, although how anyone so plain could bewitch anyone was past Kennedy's comprehension.

She heard Nicole in the kitchen, chatting quietly with James and Maddox. "Well, Maddox," Nicole said, "if you eat every bite of your sandwich, you may have a candy cane, but only if your daddy says so."

Who was Nicole to control what Kennedy's child ate? Annoyance propelled Kennedy ungracefully off the sofa.

"Mommy. Let me take you to my room so you can rest."

In the hall, Katya started to climb the stairs.

"No, wait. We're in the birthing room behind the

kitchen," Kennedy informed her mother. "So I don't have to climb the stairs all the time."

"Good idea," Katya replied. She hesitated, understandably reluctant to enter the kitchen.

Kennedy took her mother's hand and pulled her along. Nicole was at the sink, rinsing dishes before stacking them in the dishwasher. James was covering a platter of fresh veggie strips with cling wrap. Maddox sat on a chair, swinging his legs, sucking a candy cane.

"Mommy's going to take a brief nap," Kennedy proclaimed, her tone of voice leaving no room for discussion.

"I'm going to take a nap, too, Grandmama," Maddox told her.

Katya crouched down to kiss her grandson. "Have a good sleep, my angel. I'll see you later." Rising, she followed Kennedy into the birthing room.

"The bathroom's through here," Kennedy began, then stopped, blushing. "Of course you know that."

Katya looked around the room. "So Nicole changed the den into a bedroom." With a sigh, she sat down on the wide bed that, Kennedy realized with a blip of relief, she had actually made this morning. Unzipping her boots, Katya kicked them off, raised her shapely legs onto the bed, and reclined onto a pillow. "Oh, my. This feels divine."

Kennedy unfolded a patchwork quilt and spread it over Katya. She kissed her mother's forehead. "Have a good rest."

"Thank you, dear." Katya closed her eyes.

Kennedy left the room, quietly shutting the door, thinking how odd it felt to do something so maternal to her own mother.

20

❄

The boy's fort was better than nothing, but the temperature was falling while the wind rose. It was late afternoon and the boy who called him Pooh hadn't brought him anything to eat since last night when he brought out that piece of excellent meat.

He worried the boy had forgotten him. The light that came with morning was already fading. This was good for when Snix needed to sneak out of his fort and scurry over behind a bush to pee. It made him less visible to the people inside the brightly lighted house. But it was bad for finding food. So was the snow pelting down everywhere. Already it was piled so high that Snix had trouble lifting his short legs in and out of it. Once or twice he got stuck, which made him even colder. He jumped his way back into the fort, his coat covered with flakes.

He licked the icy white off his legs and shoulders and rolled on the cushions. He tried nosing a cushion up against another one to make a notch where he could wriggle down into for warmth. It didn't work very well. The wind was so strong it rattled the lawn chairs and lifted the edges of the cardboard and blankets.

He couldn't understand why the boy hadn't come back. Perhaps this was the way humans were, hugging and feeding you one day, completely forgetting you the next.

Or maybe it was that Snix was unlovable. He wasn't much to look at, he knew. He was too small to guard a house. He was too small even to make it through the increasing piles of snow to search for food. No one needed a dog like him.

His stomach growled as hunger clawed at it. He whimpered pathetically.

Wait! He heard a noise. The back door was opening. He crawled to the edge of the lawn chair tunnel and peeked out between the slats.

It wasn't the boy. Snix's heart sank.

But it was a woman carrying a heavy clear bag of garbage, and even through the blowing snow Snix could smell the layers of cooked and raw food. These people had a heavy plastic garbage can with a tight-fitting lid that clamped shut so decidedly that Snix had never been able to open it.

But he'd never been this desperate before. He would wait until the woman went back inside, then attack the garbage can with all his might.

21

❄

At preschool, everyone talked about Christmas as full of excitement, presents, good food, and fun. But Christmas was tomorrow and everyone in the house was grumpy. Maddox could *feel* the heaviness. He knew he was only a kid, he couldn't understand everything, but he knew when people bustled or whistled or sang, and right now the house was silent except for the sound of Nicole clashing pots and pans in the kitchen.

That was wrong. Nicole always fluttered around in the kitchen like a butterfly, humming to herself. Now her expression was grim. Grandmama had disappeared into the bedroom. Mommy and Daddy were in the living room, talking in low voices. Granddad sat in the kitchen nook, phoning hotels.

The windows rattled, battered by the storm. *Pooh!*, Maddox thought. Maddox hadn't been able to get outside to take him food since yesterday, because he always had a grown-up taking him here and there. The poor dog must be cold and hungry.

This might be the perfect time to sneak outside with some food. Maddox had eaten all of his grilled cheese sandwich, but the grown-ups hadn't. Nicole was piling the crusts into the trash bag now, where they joined bits of bacon, eggs, toast, and other breakfast goodies that had been left over from this morning. It would be a feast for his puppy pal!

How could he steal the bag away from Nicole? Already it looked too heavy for Maddox to carry it, but he could drag it, but not in front of the grown-ups . . . While he deliberated, Nicole swiftly twisted and tied the opening, hefted it up, and headed to the mudroom and the back door.

Disappointment flooded Maddox. He knew he wasn't strong enough to unclamp the garbage cans. But he had to be inventive, he had to be strong, he had to feed Pooh. Quickly scanning the kitchen, he discovered a box of Cheerios left on the counter. Okay, maybe dogs didn't eat Cheerios, but it was better than nothing.

Like a spy, Maddox slipped out to the mudroom, pulled on his boots, then dove beneath the bench where people sat to take off their boots or put them on. The door opened, snow gusted in on an invisible carpet of cold air, and Nicole's feet strode past, stamping snow onto the floor. She went into the kitchen.

Maddox sneaked out from under the bench. Reaching up, he turned the knob and pulled the back door open. Sliding through the smallest possible opening, he stepped out onto the back porch and pulled the door shut tight.

Light from the kitchen fell onto the porch and backyard. From here he could see how the wind buffeted the fort, clattering the cardboard against the wood and making the edges of the blankets lift and drop. Still, it stood. So Pooh was warm inside.

Maddox hurried down the steps toward the fort. Wind spun through his hair and dotted his face with snowflakes, but he was warm enough in the wool Christmas sweater Nicole had knit especially for him.

Kneeling down, he crawled through the lawn chair entrance into the fort.

"Pooh!" he called. "I'm here. I'm here, Pooh. I've brought you something to eat."

Pooh wasn't there.

22

❄

As Nicole carried out the garbage, she wondered why Sebastian was making phone calls on his ex-wife's behalf. This garbage bag was heavy, but Sebastian was too busy on the phone, helping Princess Katya. For heaven's sake, couldn't James or Kennedy or Katya herself made the calls? Were Katya's filed, French-tipped fingernails too delicate to punch numbers into a phone?

Bah, humbug, Nicole thought as she tromped up the back steps. All her visions of a lollipop Noel had fled before the nightmare of gorgeous, vulnerable Katya arriving to take over the house and the holiday.

Back in the house, she saw James secluded in the living room whispering with Kennedy. Sebastian was in the kitchen, grim-faced.

"Most of the hotels and B&Bs are closed for the season. The few that are open are booked. No rooms available." Seeing Nicole's frustration, he tried to lighten the moment. "No room at the inn."

Nicole was aware that her hair had been stirred by the wind into all kinds of crazy. She had tried to ignore the fact that her middle-aged bottom had grown bigger and rounder as she'd spent the month cooking delicacies for the holiday, but with Katya here, so slim and toned, Nicole admitted to herself that she looked like a peasant compared to a queen. No, not a peasant, a servant. The mild, self-effacing worker bee who cooked the meals, did the dishes, made the beds, and dusted and cleaned so the family, Sebastian's family, could flutter through life like the aristocrats Katya assumed they were.

Nicole lifted her hand to smooth down her hair. "Right now, at this particular moment, I'm not in the mood to be benevolent."

Sebastian swayed back, surprised. Nicole seldom spoke in this way. He apologized, "I'm sorry I didn't carry out the garbage. I know the bag was heavy."

"I'm bushed," Nicole told him, and it was true. She was at the end of her rope, which allowed all sorts of demonic phrases to pepper her mind, filling her with dark thoughts.

I'll leave. I'll go to Jilly's and let you have your perfect wife and family all back together again. Those words were on the tip of her tongue, but she knew they weren't rational, she was simply overemotional and overwhelmed. Sebastian had not done anything to make her doubt his love for her. He had stepped away when Katya tried to paw him. He had put his arm around Nicole. She had to tamp down her temper.

"I'm going upstairs to lie down," Nicole said. "I need a rest."

Her heart lightened when Sebastian said, "I'll come with you."

They lay side by side on their backs on the bed. Nicole stared at the ceiling.

Sebastian reached for Nicole's hand. "I'm sorry Katya showed up like this. She's never been considerate of other people."

"She wants you back," Nicole stated bluntly.

Sebastian rolled over and put an arm around Nicole, pulling her close to him. "I am married to you. I am in love with you." He nibbled her ear. "You and I are a team, Nicole. In a couple of days, everyone else will be gone, and you and I will have our house and our lives back to ourselves."

"Yes, but when Kennedy has her baby, you and Katya and James will be with her and I'll be exiled."

Sebastian took a deep breath. "Exiled is putting it a bit strong."

Nicole didn't speak.

"What can I do?" Sebastian asked. "It's what my daughter requested. And Katya and I are the biological grandparents." After a moment, he continued, "Give Kennedy a break. She's a good person, deep down. She's not thinking clearly. I think she's pretty overwhelmed by pregnancy hormones."

Nicole turned on her side, away from Sebastian. Truly, she was fed up with shopping, cooking, cleaning, decorating, not to mention pretending that Kennedy's little act with the photo albums hadn't wounded her. And the worst was yet to come. If Katya stayed for Christmas, how would that work? Everyone was aligned to Kennedy except Nicole, who was left out. And what about the cooking and cleaning up? If Katya didn't help, Nicole would feel like her maid. If Katya *did* help, Nicole would be painfully aware that Katya had cooked in the kitchen for years.

Tears were pressing against her chest and her eyes. "I w-wanted this to be a wonderful Christmas," she managed to stutter.

"What can I do to help?" Sebastian repeated. "There must be something."

Why couldn't Sebastian just *know*? Nicole struggled for an answer. "Be with me," she told him. "Don't let Katya touch you. Don't respond to her flirting. Make it clear that this is *our* house now, your house and mine."

Sebastian cuddled her against him. "I'll do that. And remember, Nicole, Katya and I were estranged even before the divorce. She pretty much lived in the Boston house while I preferred to live here. I was relieved when she ran off with Alonzo—but I've told you all this before."

Reassured by the warmth of his arms and his words, Nicole agreed, "Okay. I can do this. If you're by my side."

"Don't worry, I'm right here." Sebastian hugged her tightly.

Yet Nicole knew that, for her, Christmas was ruined.

23

❄

Kennedy could not get comfortable on the living room sofa. She had eaten too much of Nicole's amazingly delicious food. Rubbing her hands over her swollen belly, she closed her eyes and tried to relax, but thoughts of her mother stirred through her emotions. As much as Kennedy had hated it when her mother divorced her father, she had been glad for Katya whenever Katya was with Alonzo, because this new love had made Katya glitter in ways Kennedy had never seen before. Katya had acted silly, hugging and smooching Kennedy with a carefree, spontaneous enthusiasm that was entirely new.

Now Alonzo and Katya were over. Kennedy could tell her mother was hurting more than she let others see. The fact that Katya wanted to take a nap? *Whoa.* Katya had never taken naps before.

James was outside, shoveling the walk and the drive.

The sound of the blade hitting the bricks made Kennedy grit her teeth. Couldn't he wait?

If only Nicole would just *leave*. Then Kennedy's father wouldn't have to behave so dutifully to his new wife. Sebastian would be free to gaze upon Katya with clear eyes, he would see that they belonged together, he would take her in his arms, and everyone in the house would belong.

24

❄

"Pooh!" Maddox struggled through the back yard, following the bumpy path through the snow toward the garage. "Pooh! Where are you?"

The snow reached the top of his boots. The wind pushed at him, and snow swirled up his nose. Fear burned his heart, shame sliced his belly. He should have brought the puppy some food this morning. If Pooh had run away because he thought Maddox had abandoned him . . . Maddox sobbed aloud. The sound flew away in the storm.

It wasn't quite dark yet. Lights from the house fell over the yard, and as Maddox went around the side of the garage, his heart exploded with gladness. There he was! The little terrier was standing on his hind legs, trying to push over the heavy garbage container, which rocked but did not fall.

"Pooh!"

The dog turned, saw Maddox, and, yelping jubilantly,

bounded through the few feet between them, throwing himself at Maddox with delirium. Maddox put his arms around the animal. Pooh was shivering. Pooh whined with ecstasy, licking Maddox's face with an icy tongue.

"You're going inside with me," Maddox told the animal.

He tried to pick Pooh up in his arms, and he did manage it, but the dog's weight made Maddox almost fall over backward. Heroically, Maddox toiled forward, one step at a time, through the mountains of white. The dog rested his head on Maddox's shoulder. It was the most wonderful feeling. Keeping to the jagged path he had broken through on his way out, he managed to labor his way right up to the steps to the back porch. Here, he collapsed, out of breath.

"Pooh," he gasped, setting the dog down next to him.

Pooh squeezed as close to Maddox as he could. They were both quaking with cold.

Maddox stood up. His snowboots were warm, but they were heavy. He'd be glad to get them off. Resolutely, he climbed the wooden steps.

"Come on, Pooh," he called. The dog leapt up the steps, right alongside Maddox.

Maddox reached way up to turn the doorknob. He shoved the door open. Warmth flooded out from the mudroom.

"Come on, Pooh," he called again.

Pooh didn't hesitate. He bounced across the porch and into the house. Maddox pulled the door shut. In the bright light, he saw how each individual hair on Pooh's body was crusted with snow. It frosted poor Pooh's nose and the tips of his ears. Maddox seized his own navy blue coat with the red plaid lining and wrapped it over the dog, holding him tightly.

"Maddox!" Suddenly Grandmama Katya loomed in the doorway, looking cross and even kind of mean. "What is *that?*"

25

❄

Snix nestled his head on the boy's shoulder, savoring this surprising moment of belonging. He was wanted. He was *chosen*. He was very nearly warm.

And he'd bet the little boy would feed him any minute now. His stomach rumbled hungrily. He hoped the boy could feel it.

The boy's arms tightened around Snix when the thin blond woman came into the mudroom. Snix felt him tense up. He could smell the woman's scent, much like cat pee, and the boy's anxiety. Snix stayed still, sensing it was a good time to be invisible.

The woman kept saying *Maddox*. Maddox must be the boy's name. Good to know.

"Santa brought him to me," Maddox told the woman.

She laughed, but the sound wasn't lighthearted. "Maddox, Christmas isn't until tomorrow, *darling*. Besides, dogs aren't allowed in the house."

Maddox's arms were trembling from supporting Snix's weight. Squatting down, he put Snix on the floor. He removed his coat from Snix's body. "He's just a *little* dog," Maddox pointed out.

Snix tried to squeeze himself small. He lay down on the floor—the soft rag rug felt good against his belly—and put his head between his paws.

"I don't care what size the animal is. Dogs are not allowed in this house."

"*Excuse me?*" Another woman entered the mudroom. This one didn't smell like cat pee. She smelled wonderful. She smelled like food. "Oh, Maddox, who is this?"

Food Woman knelt next to Snix. Snix lifted his head hopefully. Food Woman slowly reached out to let Snix smell her hand, a true courtesy, then gently scratched him behind his ears.

"Hello, cutie-pie. What's your name?"

In reply, Snix licked her wrist, perhaps a bit too enthusiastically, but it was ringed with the slight aroma of melted cheese.

"Pooh," Maddox told Food Woman. "I've named him Pooh."

"Well, Pooh, you appear just a tad bedraggled. I'll bet you'd like something to eat. Perhaps a nice bowl of warm milk and a bit of—"

"Don't tell me you intend to feed that creature!" Blond

Woman was indignant. "If you do that, you'll never get rid of him."

"Santa brought him!" Maddox protested, getting to his feet. "He did, Nicole!"

"Dogs are not allowed in this house," Blond Woman said, her voice as cold as the wind outside.

Food Woman spoke, her voice low, vibrating with indignation. "May I remind you, you do not make the rules here. This is not your house any longer."

"Mommy!" shouted Maddox as another woman squeezed her bulk into the room. She was young and pretty and hugely fat.

"What's wrong? Maddox, what have you done?"

"Mommy." Maddox babbled, suddenly crouching over Snix. "Santa left me this dog. I want to keep him. His name is Pooh. He won't eat much."

Actually . . . Snix thought, almost dizzy with hunger and the enticing bouquet of beef, cheese, and oatmeal . . .

His thoughts were interrupted. "I've told you, Maddox, you can't have a pet. I'm sorry, but we're going to have a new baby soon."

"But, Mommy—" Maddox argued, stamping his foot.

"MADDOX, you are being a very BAD boy!" his mother yelled.

"Then *I'll* keep him," Food Woman announced.

"You will *not*!" Blond Woman bristled with outrage.

"An animal will ruin this house! The floors will be scratched, the furniture ripped to shreds—"

"As I said," Food Woman replied calmly, "this is not your house."

Maddox's mommy turned bright red and stuck her face into Food Woman's face. "How dare you be rude to my mother!"

"What's going on?" An older man came into the room, which made the mudroom crowded.

"Daddy!" the fat lady with the bulging tummy cried.

"Sebastian," Blond Woman said and at the same time, Food Woman said, "Sebastian."

Everyone talked at once, which made it possible for Maddox to pick his coat off the floor, toss it over Snix, clutch Snix to his chest, push open the back door, and run back out into the cold.

26

❄

"Tell her, Daddy, *tell* her!" Kennedy threw herself into her father's arms. Tears flew from her eyes. "Tell Nicole she is not allowed to make rules for *my* son!"

"I didn't—" Nicole began.

"Kennedy?" James came into the room. He'd finished shoveling the front walk, and snow topped his wool hat and the shoulders of his coat. "What's going on?"

Kennedy could hardly remain standing. She was out of breath, overwhelmed by the situation, bent in half by her emotions.

Katya spoke, her voice laced with contempt for Nicole. "Nicole thinks she can tell Kennedy how to run her life."

"No, I do not," Nicole disagreed, almost spitting each word.

Kennedy shuddered. "Daddy, make her stop being mean to Mommy."

"Kennedy." James stepped forward and put his hand on her shoulder. "Honey, what's gotten into you? You sound like a whining adolescent."

Nicole folded her arms in the most *satisfied* way. Kennedy wanted to *slap* her.

"Don't you speak to my daughter that way!" Katya snapped.

"Why don't we all calm down," Sebastian suggested. "Let's get out of the mudroom and discuss this reasonably."

"Discuss *what*?" James asked.

"Nicole wants to let Maddox keep the dog," Kennedy told him.

"What dog?" James asked.

Kennedy shrieked. "WHERE'S MADDOX?"

Silence suddenly filled the mudroom as everyone turned to stare at the place where the boy and dog had been standing. Now there was only a wet spot on the rug and a small pile of melting snow.

Sebastian strode across the empty space, yanked open the back door, and yelled out into the dark night: "Maddox? Maddox!"

Nicole hurried to his side. Stepping out onto the back porch, she called, "Maddox, honey, it's okay. The dog can come in, too."

"How dare she," Katya muttered.

Sebastian took a flashlight from the shelf above the coat hooks and hurried out into the yard. "Maddox? Maddox!"

"Maybe he's in his fort." Nicole trotted down the back steps and through the snowdrifts, fell to her knees, and crawled inside the lawn chair tunnel. After a moment, she backed out. "They're not in there."

Kennedy's heart seemed to explode with anguish. "What have I done?" Snatching the first coat her hand found, she pulled it over her shoulders.

As Kennedy wobbled out onto the porch and down the steps, her mother shouted, "Kennedy! You can't go out in this weather. Not in your shape. You'll fall! Kennedy, get back in here."

James brushed past his mother-in-law, rushed out the back door, and caught Kennedy as she reached the bottom step. "Kennedy," he crooned. "It's okay." Taking a moment, he stroked the side of her face with his hand.

James's caring touch, his concerned gaze, soothed Kennedy. For a second, in the midst of the swirling snow, the world made sense.

"James," she sobbed. "I was mean to Maddox. He wants to keep a puppy he found and I said he couldn't. He said Santa brought it to him. I said . . ." She couldn't finish. She hated herself at that moment. She was the worst mother in the world. "I told Maddox he was *bad*. On

Christmas Eve. So he ran away." She bent over double with pain.

James wrapped his arms around her tight. He was so strong. His love for her was a healing balm. "Let's get you back inside. You need to take care of yourself. I'll go find Maddox. He can't have gone far."

Sebastian and Nicole approached, ghostly in their snow-covered clothing.

"He's not in the yard or garage or at the front of the house," Sebastian announced.

Kennedy choked back a sob.

27

❄

Nicole had a sudden thought. "Maybe he went up to his room. I'll check." She raced out of the mudroom, through the front hall, and up the stairs. The door to Maddox's room was open. The room was empty.

"He's not there," she called as she hurried back down the stairs.

"We're going to look for him," Sebastian yelled.

"We'll find him!" James promised desperately. The two men hurried out.

The front door slammed. Nicole hesitated in the hallway, wondering whether she should join the search party, too.

Just then, to her great surprise, there came from the mudroom an extended, anguished, guttural bellow. It was a sound Nicole knew well from her days as a nurse. She closed her eyes and took a deep breath.

Katya was helping Kennedy into the front hall.

Katya looked exasperated. "For heaven's sake, Kennedy, enough with the melodrama. They'll find him."

Nicole said, "It's not melodrama, Katya. Your daughter's in labor."

"Don't be ridiculous," Katya countered.

Kennedy was almost crouching, hands on the wall for support.

Nicole went to the young woman. "Let's go into the living room. It's the warmest room in the house. I'll check your contractions."

Unable to speak, Kennedy allowed Nicole to support her as they slowly made their way into the living room. A fire flickered brightly in the fireplace, and the Christmas tree glittered in the window.

"Put your hands on the back of the chair," Nicole told Kennedy.

Kennedy leaned on the armchair with Nicole standing behind her. Suddenly, a gush of blood-tinged water flooded from her body.

"Kennedy! What are you doing? The rug is Turkish!" Katya cried.

Nicole ignored the other woman, her hands on Kennedy's belly.

"Katya, the baby is coming. Call 911."

"The baby isn't due for three more weeks," Katya argued, adding, "Maddox was ten days late."

Kennedy was growling constantly now. Digging her hands into the back of the chair for support, she gasped, "Mommy. *Call 911.*"

With a sniff, Katya took her cellphone out of the pocket of her cashmere skirt and punched in the numbers. She punched them in again. She looked at the phone, mystified. "It's dead. My cell is dead."

"Try the landline," Nicole told her. "In the kitchen."

"Oooooooooh." Kennedy's legs were shaking. "Nicole, I think I'm having the baby."

"Yes. I think you are, too. Don't worry, Kennedy. You'll be fine."

Kennedy lifted her face to the ceiling, straining. A long wail tore from her body.

Katya ran in from the kitchen. "That line's dead, too."

"Must be the storm," Nicole murmured, preoccupied.

"Kennedy, are you okay?" Katya's splendid forehead wrinkled in concern.

Nicole calmly informed her: "Katya, she's having the baby. Now."

Katya opened her mouth to object, but her daughter's moans drove the reality past her doubts. "Dear Lord. What can we do?"

Nicole guided Katya's hands onto Kennedy's waist. "Hold Kennedy. Support her from behind. It's good that she's standing. Gravity will help the baby come down the birth canal."

"Where are you going?" Katya shrieked, her voice shrill with fear.

"To scrub up. I'll get some scissors, twine, and towels."

Katya went white. "I'm going to faint."

"Not now you're not," Nicole said in a tone that brooked no disagreement. She hurried from the room.

In the kitchen, she quickly, knowledgeably, gathered the things she needed. She dashed into the guest room to collect a pile of towels and pillows. She scrubbed her hands with hot water and soap, then raced back into the living room, where Kennedy was roaring in pain while Katya held her daughter up. It was impossible to guess which woman was trembling the most.

Nicole knelt behind Kennedy and lifted the skirt of her red dress, tucking it into the neck. She sliced off Kennedy's sodden maternity panties.

"Kennedy. I'm going to check how far down your baby has come."

"I can't do this!" Kennedy howled. "Give me something for the pain! Please!"

"Whiskey? Brandy?" Katya offered helpfully. "I have some Advil in my travel kit."

With expert gentleness, Nicole put one hand on Kennedy's hip, and with the other hand, she slowly explored the birth canal, delicately moving her hand up. She felt the head. As always, this first touch filled her with wonder and gratitude.

"Kennedy. Your baby's almost here."

Kennedy screamed. "Please! It hurts too much! I can't!"

Katya was weeping. "Help her, Nicole. Do something."

"Do you think you can move to the coffee table?" Nicole asked.

"Are you mad?" Katya asked. "The coffee table isn't long enough for her to—"

"I don't want her to lie down on it. I want her to lean her arms on it. I don't think she can stand up much longer."

Gasping, crimson-faced, Kennedy managed the few awkward steps, supported by her mother and Nicole.

Nicole swept the bronze bowl of nuts off onto the floor and tossed a pillow in its place. She helped Kennedy lower herself so that each knee was on a pillow and her arms and upper body were supported by the table. She put another pillow between Kennedy's legs.

"Oh, God!" Kennedy shrieked. "The baby's coming! The baby's coming! I can feel him coming!"

"Kennedy, listen to me. I want you to take a deep breath. When I say, I want you to push."

"What can *I* do?" Katya wrung her hands with worry.

"Go around to the other side of the table. Hold Kennedy's shoulders. Hold her tight when she pushes."

Katya did as Nicole said, kneeling on the floor among the flung walnuts, putting her hands on Kennedy's shoulders.

"Now, Kennedy, *push*," Nicole said.

Kennedy gripped her mother's arms and pushed down so fiercely her body shuddered with the effort. When she stopped, she collapsed against the pillow on the coffee table, gasping for breath, too drained to speak.

28

❄

"Okay, Kennedy. Again. *Push*."

Kennedy pushed. She felt a force helping her. Her mother was helping her, holding on to her shoulders with a strength Kennedy never knew Katya had. Nicole was helping her. Nicole was a calm blur of movement and words, a serious, capable, confident strength. Something else possessed Kennedy now, a formidable, irresistible power that filled Kennedy's body like water rushing into a vessel.

She pushed, lowing like a beast.

Pain tore through her. Something ripped inside her. She bellowed.

"Your baby's crowned," Nicole said. "One more push and he's here."

Shuddering, lost to the world, surrendering to what she could not evade, Kennedy yowled and pushed. The pain was unbearable—and then it diminished. She sagged against the coffee table, broken, mute, and helpless.

Behind her, Nicole was moving rapidly. "Come over here, Katya," she directed. "Give me the twine. Cut it here. Tie it here. Okay, now cut."

"Oh, God," Katya wept. "Oh, God, oh, God, oh God. Kennedy, you have a baby!"

Kennedy could only keen as she felt the placenta move through her, carrying more pain along with it.

"Kennedy, we're going to help you lie down now," Nicole said. "Katya, pile those pillows on the floor. Kennedy, you're going to rest against the pillows so we can put your daughter in your arms."

Through the fog of shimmering fatigue, one word stood out, in startling, terrifying bluntness. When the ultrasound was done months ago, the technician had told them the baby was a boy.

"Something's wrong with the baby," Kennedy sobbed.

Katya and Nicole laughed together.

"Nothing's wrong with your baby," Nicole insisted. "Now I'm going to help you lie down. Come on, lean on me, I can take your weight, we're going to turn a bit . . . there. More comfortable?"

Kennedy's eyes cleared as her weight was supported by the cushions behind her. She saw her mother kneeling next to her, holding a naked baby in her arms.

"Kennedy, she's a little girl." Katya lowered the baby into Kennedy's eager arms.

The baby was magenta-pink, covered with white wax, peeping like a bird, waving its arms and legs. Kennedy checked: yes, she was absolutely a little girl. The most beautiful little girl in the world.

"Oh, my baby darling," Kennedy cooed softly.

The baby turned her face toward Kennedy, instinctively settling into Kennedy's arms, against her breasts.

Kennedy looked up at Nicole. "Is she healthy? Does she have everything?"

Nicole was weeping and laughing at the same time. "She's perfect. She has everything. She doesn't even seem underweight. And she's long. Look how long her legs are. She's got her all her toes, fingernails, eyebrows—she's absolutely complete."

"She's beautiful," Kennedy whispered.

"She is. As soon as we can get hold of a doctor, or get over to the hospital, we'll get some antibiotic ointment to put in her eyes." Nicole held up her hand. "It's state law. It's done for all babies at birth, to prevent infection, but it doesn't have to be done immediately, it can wait, don't worry."

Kennedy couldn't stop staring at the tiny creature in her arms, so strange, so unknown, so entirely, absolutely belonging to her.

"Katya," Nicole said, "could you please get something

clean and warm for Kennedy? Something soft, that opens in the front? Perhaps a cotton robe?"

"I don't want to leave the baby," Katya confessed with tears in her eyes.

Nicole laughed. "She'll be here when you get back. Go to my room. My softest old robe is tossed over a chair." Nicole bent over Kennedy. "I want to wrap your baby in this towel for warmth, then I'll give her back to you."

Kennedy was vaguely aware of her mother leaving the room. When Nicole lifted the baby away from her, Kennedy realized how uncomfortable she was, and how soggy the towels were beneath her bum.

"Am I okay?" she asked. She realized she was shaking.

"You're fine. Childbirth is a messy business." As she spoke, Nicole wrapped the baby and placed her back in Kennedy's arms. "You're trembling because you've just had a baby. It's normal."

Katya returned with the white terry cloth robe.

"Help your daughter put it on," Nicole said. Once again, she took the baby.

Kennedy groaned as she struggled to sit up. Her mother knelt behind her, unzipping her red dress and pulling it up over her head. She unsnapped the maternity bra, which was wet with sweat, and swiftly patted Kennedy's neck and back with a towel before helping her slip her arms into the downy robe. Katya's delicate ministrations released memories of her long-ago childhood, when her mother had helped her dress. As her mind cleared of pain, a kind of bliss replaced it at the thought of such care, such tenderness.

"Do you think you could stand up?" Nicole asked. "You'd be more comfortable on the sofa."

Kennedy nodded. With her mother's help, she shoved herself into a standing position. Fluids ran down her legs. "Sorry," Kennedy said. "Gross."

Nicole chuckled. "Natural." With another towel, she dried Kennedy's legs.

Katya supported Kennedy as she limped toward the sofa. "Don't fall on the nuts."

"Now why do I find that statement humorous?" Nicole wondered aloud with a grin. She was layering the sofa with more towels and plumping up pillows, working with ease and efficiency with the baby tucked in one arm.

"I need a pad between my legs," Kennedy said.

Nicole paused. "I don't have any."

"I haven't had any for some time," Katya said.

The two women looked at each other and a comradely expression of relief mixed with regret passed between them.

"Well, I certainly haven't needed any for months," Kennedy told them.

"A towel will work," Nicole decided.

Kennedy lowered herself onto the sofa, which took her weight like a mound of clouds. Her mother arranged the robe over her legs. Nicole laid the baby in her arms. Kennedy gazed down at the pink, serene, wondering face, a face completely radiant with trust. Someone, her mother or Nicole, tucked a warm blanket around her, and Kennedy thought what a blessing it was to have that, just that, a person who covers you with a blanket and tucks it around you with care. Right now, it seemed a good reason to be born.

29

❄

Maddox ran and ran. He ran down the block and around the corner before he had to stop to catch his breath. Setting Pooh down, he huffed, “Don’t run away.”

The little dog cocked his head, wagged his tail, and scooted next to Maddox’s leg.

At the other end of the street, a group of people were coming out of a restaurant, guffawing, hugging, patting one another on the shoulders. The sight and sounds encouraged Maddox, drew him toward them.

It was cold. Maddox glanced at Pooh. “You have fur,” he reasoned. “I don’t. I’ll hold you if you get cold, okay?”

Pooh wagged his tail, so Maddox took his coat off the puppy and slipped his own arms into it. The warmth was immediate and wonderful.

“Come on, Pooh,” Maddox said, lifting his chin and setting out optimistically, kicking his way through the snow. “Maybe we’ll find some nice people with a cellphone. They can call Daddy and Mommy and then . . ."

His imagination took him no further. He would get there and see what happened next. They would be sorry, his parents, especially his mommy, who had screamed at him in the most terrible voice he had ever heard, as if she hated him, as if she had turned into one of those monsters on the games big boys played. At the memory, his eyes welled with tears. He had *not* been such a bad boy. He'd done worse things before. He'd spilled stuff and been sassy, and he wasn't good at sharing.

Maybe his mommy would be glad he had left.

Pooh slipped and slid along next to Maddox as he walked down the middle of the street. Plows and sanders had come through, so this road was clear, although snow continued to fall, turning to ice as it landed.

Still, Maddox was walking toward the center of town, which blazed with lights, providing a sort of warmth in his heart. By the time he got to the restaurant, the group of people were getting into cars and driving away, so he kept on walking, hands in his pocket, twisting his mouth around as he pondered what to do.

The bookstore was open. He saw people moving around inside.

"Come on, Pooh," he said, reaching way up for the handle on the door.

They stepped into a pool of summer. Merriment, chatter, and delicious warm air. Maddox stood by the door a moment, just savoring the heat, aware of his dog leaning on his ankle.

"We're closing!" someone called out.

Adults, all of them very tall, crowded and jostled to get to the counter with their last-minute purchases. One of them trod on Pooh's foot. Pooh yipped in surprise. The tall man glowered down at Maddox.

"Does that animal bite?"

"No," Maddox began. "We need—"

But the man turned away, moving up in line. A woman with boots like his mommy wore, with long pointed dagger-like heels, stepped near Pooh, who cowered closer to Maddox.

Dismayed, Maddox picked Pooh up in his arms, pushed the door open, and went back outside. He didn't want Pooh to get stabbed in the foot. He plodded down the street, lugging Pooh in his arms.

A sudden melancholy fell over him. By now his daddy should be running down the street, yelling for him, calling, "Come back, Maddox! We'll let you keep the dog!"

His stomach growled. His arms hurt. He set Pooh down on the icy sidewalk. Pooh tilted his head questioningly.

"I'm hungry, Pooh, and I'll bet you are, too." Maddox sniffed the air. No smells lured him forward.

He didn't know where to go or what to do. He'd run away full of pride and courage and filled with a sense of adventure. Now he knew he was only a cold, hungry, helpless boy.

30

❄

His boy paused on the corner. Not the smartest thing to do, Pooh thought, because the wind howled so fiercely it almost knocked Maddox over. When they were walking, their momentum carried them forward into the wind, or the wind pushed them along, but standing made Pooh shudder with cold.

He was so hungry he wanted to whimper with misery. Yet he was so overjoyed that Maddox had taken him that his misery was offset. Mostly. His belly still rumbled and complained, as if it hadn't yet received the news of his good luck.

He peered up at the boy's face, searching for a clue to his mood. Where would they go next? The boy, although young and small, was a human, with access to doors in many warm places. He was smart and resourceful, too. After all, he'd built that warm fort.

Pooh allowed himself a moment—since Maddox was

still standing there like a lump—to puzzle over the mysterious ways of humans. He knew they couldn't be trusted; Cota Collins and her family had taught him that. He had been so sure that she loved him that he hadn't even known she could *stop* loving him. Perhaps, somehow, the fault was his.

But he believed Maddox loved him. Maddox had taken him. Maddox was with him now. And Maddox was certainly lovable, such a smart, valiant boy whose plump fingers were magnificent at scratching behind Pooh's ears.

The mystery was: Why were all those humans so terrible to each other? In the midst of this black, frightening night, they were inside a warm, bright house with the swooningly good aromas of delicious food all around them. They had a *family*, and for a moment a memory flickered in Pooh's mind, of a time when he was new, snuggling with a bunch of other squirming puppies, being licked by his mother, who looked just like him and smelled of warm milk. He remembered how his eyes opened more every day, how he wobbled around the cardboard box, learning his legs, clumsily stumbling into the other puppies—he remembered his brothers' and sisters' sharp tiny teeth! How they had rough-and-tumbled with one another, play-growling and snapping and pouncing.

He remembered how they were released out into the

yard one spring morning when the grass was fragrant and the sun fell benevolently on his back. The world surprised him, it was so enormous and bright. He would run back to his mother, to be sure she was still there, then trot back to play with his siblings.

One day, Cota came. She had picked him up, hugged him to her chest, stroked his fur, whispered lovingly into his ear.

He'd never seen his siblings or his mommy again. He'd entirely lost the trail of their odor.

Would Maddox leave him, too?

His boy's words broke into his thoughts. "Look, Pooh. We can get warm." Maddox marched bravely forward, slipping on the occasional icy patch, lifting his feet high over drifts that had avoided the shopkeepers' shovels.

Pooh struggled along behind, leaping, sliding, trotting, limping—ice had frozen between his toes, slicing the pads of his paws.

They progressed up the sidewalk, their way lighted by the small twinkling Christmas trees, toward the giant tree at the top of Main, the one in front of the brick building. Even this mammoth evergreen swayed from the force of the wind.

"Here!" Maddox shouted.

Snow blew into his eyes. Pooh blinked, then saw it. In

front of the wide white Methodist church, on the snow-covered front lawn, stood a funny structure: a three-sided shed golden with light. A spotlight was aimed at it, making the interior blaze, and on top of the shed was another light in the shape of a star.

Inside were people and a donkey. Pooh lifted his lip to growl a warning, but as they got nearer, he realized something was off about the other creatures. They weren't the right size. They didn't smell. Ah, they were statues. A father, a mother, a baby in a cradle, and the donkey.

But on the floor of the shed was real straw. Thick, golden straw.

Pooh felt himself lifted up into Maddox's arms. The boy shoved through the snow and into the shed. They were warmer immediately, from the spotlight.

"We'll stay here," Maddox told Pooh. The boy wriggled down at the back of the shed, holding Pooh close to his stomach, and used his hand to rake straw over their legs and torsos.

Warmer and warmer. The wind buffeted the sides of the shed, but it stood firm.

"We'll be safe here," Maddox assured Pooh.

Pooh yipped once, lightly, in agreement. He arched his head so he could lick Maddox's hands, which were red with cold.

"We'll rest and keep warm while I think what to do next," Maddox decided.

Pooh snuggled as close to the boy as he could. The wonderful warmth made him drowsy. But the hunger cramping his belly kept him awake.

31

❄

The living room was toasty. Nicole added logs to the fire and stirred it with the poker. The Christmas tree lights threw off a bit of heat, and of course the furnace was on.

Kennedy and her baby girl were ensconced on the sofa, covered and wrapped with blankets. Katya was performing the unthinkable: Down on her hands and knees, she crawled around the floor, picking up walnuts and replacing them in the bronze bowl.

Nicole gathered up the pile of bloodstained towels. "I'll get these into the washing machine."

"Oh, thank you, Nicole," Kennedy said. "I don't want Maddox to be frightened when he comes in and sees so much blood."

Katya frowned. "The carpet is still stained. Plus, it reeks." Suddenly, her legs buckled and she sat down, hard, on the floor. Her face was white. Her eyes were wide, her pupils dilated.

"Mommy?" Kennedy asked. "Are you okay?"

Katya said, "You had a baby." Tilting her face up toward Nicole, she gasped, "My God. What would we have done if you hadn't been here? Nicole, how can I ever thank you? I'm so grateful." She raised her hands to her face. Her shoulders shook. She made a noise that in any other woman would be considered blubbering.

Nicole bent over and wrapped her arms around Katya. "You're in shock. Let's get you in a chair. Come on, right here, where you can see Kennedy and the baby. You would have been fine without me," she assured Katya. "It's all very dramatic, isn't it?" She helped Katya stand on her shaking legs and stagger into a chair.

"Thank you, Nicole." Katya gripped Nicole's arm. "Truly. Thank you. I am full of admiration."

"You're welcome. I'm glad to be part of it all." She could tell that this was getting to be a bit more sentimental than Katya could easily deal with. "I'll be right back."

She left the room, lugging the heavy soggy towels. Even after a washing, they would be pretty much shot for normal use. She'd keep them in the mudroom for people to wipe off their shoes. She dumped them into the washing machine, added detergent, and turned the dial.

Then she leaned against the quietly humming machine, relaxed, and prayed. She prayed with gratitude for this new healthy baby, for Kennedy's quick and relatively painless labor and birthing, and she sent selfish words of thankfulness that everything had gone so well with Nicole at the receiving end. If anything had gone wrong, and things could have, Nicole would have been blamed. She would have blamed herself. She was always filled with both anticipation and anxiety when a mother gave birth, but this had been an extraordinary situation. Now she was completely out of gas. She could lie down right there on the mudroom floor and take a snooze.

Instead, she went into the kitchen to brew fresh pots of coffee and hot chocolate.

32

❄

First, Maddox just lay there, catching his breath, allowing the warmth to sink into his body like melted butter on toast. (Cinnamon toast would be excellent right now.)

He'd never been so cold before, and the cold had made him frightened and confused. Standing on the street corner with the wind shoving him in the back like a giant saying *Go away, you're not wanted here*, he'd wished with all his heart to hear his father call him, to hear running footsteps, to be swept up into loving arms. He'd stood there, waiting, listening, hoping . . . and no one came.

His mother had warned him. "Don't leave my side," she always said when they were in a store. "Don't leave the yard on your own. It's easy to get lost."

He had disobeyed her. His mommy often said, "*Now* look what happened!" when he'd done something wrong.

Now look what happened.

Out in the freezing dark, he'd been scared, shaking

with cold and fright. Here, nestled in the sweet-smelling straw with Pooh's tiny body snuggled next to him, Maddox's spirits lifted. Even though there was no wall in front, it was still like being in a house. There was light from the spotlight. There were other people, too, kind of. Even if they were only statues, he felt less alone.

One problem: no food. Of course there wasn't any food, the statues of Mary, Joseph, and baby Jesus didn't require food.

He scrabbled in his pants pockets to see if he had any candy canes left, even a broken piece. But no. He'd eaten every bite. Hugging Pooh to him, he realized the dog was probably hungry, too. Pooh was so skinny. But what a good, loyal, friend! Maddox would *never* throw Pooh out into the cold night.

So he couldn't go home. Could he? If he went back, would they allow him to keep Pooh in the house just for a while?

If he tried, could he find his way back? He thought so. Granddad's house was right up the street from the big brick Jared Coffin House, and that wasn't far away, was it?

Next to him, Pooh began to snore, a sweet rumbling sound that made Maddox grin. Relaxing into the straw, he realized he was awfully tired from all that running and carrying Pooh. Being warm made him drowsy.

A stick of straw poked his ear. He moved his head, trying to get comfortable, and sort of sat up, and sort of scanned the streets outside in case his daddy was out there looking for him.

The street was empty, except for the blowing snow.

His lower lip quivered. Tears filled his eyes. Sadness filled his heart. Snot filled his nose—unattractive, his mommy usually told him. He couldn't help it, though. He was scared.

33

❄

The baby slept, but Kennedy was a bubbling emotional geyser threatening to erupt momentarily.

She had a daughter. Joy!

Then terror blasted through her. *Maddox.* Her little boy.

Maddox had run away because she had been horrid to him. Shame, anguish, mommy guilt of the most torturous kind.

She'd given birth without James present. Heartbreak, disappointment, more guilt—couldn't she have waited?

Her mother had been present. Nicole had been helpful. Okay, more than helpful. Nicole had taken charge and conducted the entire chaotic mess with as much expertise as anyone could wish for. She had been an angel of kindness. More guilt, because Kennedy had been such a beast to Nicole.

Her mother was on the floor again with more towels,

soaking up the natural but still rather gruesome muck of childbirth. That in itself—her mother performing manual labor—filled Kennedy with incredulity. Katya did not enjoy housework. Never had. But Katya was humming a Christmas carol, and she looked exultant. Kennedy was confused.

Most of all, where was Maddox? Shouldn't her father and James have found her child and brought him back? She didn't want her son to believe that she'd blithely forgotten about him, or worse, tossed him away—"You're a bad boy!"—then lay down and gotten herself another child. Her heart wrung with worry. She was glad to have a daughter, but so frightened for Maddox.

Was this family life at its most basic? A cauldron of constantly changing sensations? Kennedy was stunned to realize that she'd been in labor all day without realizing it because she'd been so overwhelmed with intense and often ungenerous emotions. How had her own mother maneuvered through family life so serenely, like a sailboat on a windless sea? How would Kennedy survive her own family life, especially if she was as self-centered and myopic as she'd been with little Maddox?

Her sweet little boy, her darling child, with his giggle, his innocence, his wide-eyed trust in his mommy. Her heart broke when she thought of the radiant confidence on his face when he watched her. She knew she'd been cranky with him lately, restless and uncomfortable in her own body. She'd tried to explain that to him, but how could a four-year-old possibly comprehend the discomfort of a pregnant woman? She'd been mad to think he could. She'd been awful to call him a bad boy. She'd been so out of her mind she hadn't even realized she was in labor.

Kennedy was mortified. Here she was, tucked up with her new baby in her arms, warm and well-cared-for, and her precious son was out there in the bitter stormy night. She should search for him. She struggled to sit up. Not a good idea.

"Mommy?" she quavered.

Katya responded instantly. "Yes, sweetie?"

"Would you help James and Daddy search for Maddox? I'm so afraid. They should be back with him by now."

Katya hesitated. "Of course I'll go. But someone should stay with you. Would you rather Nicole searched and I stayed?"

Her mother's words appeared to be free of judgment.

"I suppose since Nicole's a nurse, and the baby is so new, and I'm still a bit of a mess . . ." Kennedy let her voice trail off.

"You're right." Katya rose to her feet. "I'll put on my coat and help look for Maddox. Don't worry, darling. We'll find him."

"Thank you, Mommy." Kennedy began to cry. What if

they didn't find him? What if he was hiding in the dark garage of a summer family who had gone away? What if he developed pneumonia or hypothermia?

What if Maddox thought no one was looking for him? What if he thought that because she'd told him he was bad, she no longer loved him? She imagined her son cold, lost, and frightened, and sobs broke out, startling her newborn babe. But she couldn't stop crying.

34

❄

Nicole entered the living room to find Katya with her own arms full of stained cloths and towels.

"I got it as dry as I could." Katya stared ruefully at the stained rug.

"It's fine," Nicole told her. "The heat of the fire will dry it, and we'll toss a throw rug over it. In fact, I know just the one. It's a Christmas rug my grandmother hooked for me, with snowmen and decorations on it."

Katya, who had obviously recovered from her sentimental moment, looked horrified.

"Maddox will like it," Nicole reminded her. "He'll think it's a decoration and won't know what it's hiding."

"Mommy's going to go look for Maddox," Kennedy said from the sofa. She was weeping steadily. "They should be back by now."

Nicole set the tray of warm drinks on the coffee table.

Squeezing onto the sofa next to Kennedy, she lifted the young woman's arm and put her fingers on her wrist, taking her pulse.

"You're fine, Kennedy. I'm sure Maddox is fine, too. He can't have gone far. The three of us need to take a moment to settle down. We've all been part of a momentous occasion. Let's have some coffee—hot chocolate for you, Kennedy. If they're still not back by the time we've finished our drinks, Katya or I can go out and look, too." She handed the drinks around.

Katya was content to let Nicole take charge. She sipped her coffee, so rich and fragrant, with the kick of Bailey's in it. "Alcohol?"

Nicole nodded. "For medicinal purposes," she said, not quite joking. She took a restoring sip of her own coffee.

Katya peered over at her granddaughter, tucked securely in Kennedy's arms. "What is she doing?"

"She's sleeping," Kennedy said. Glancing at Nicole, she asked, "That's okay, right?"

"That's absolutely okay. She's probably tired, too. She's just been born. She's warm, she can smell her mommy, you're holding her next to your heart so she can hear it beating, she's exactly where she should be."

"If only Maddox were here," Kennedy wept. "Today's been such a *jumble*. I feel like I've done everything wrong.

I can't even love this new baby as much as I should because I'm so frightened for Maddox."

Katya chuckled. "Mommy fear. It's the worst. I used to be terrified when you took gymnastics. I often had to leave the meet to throw up."

"I never knew that," Kennedy said.

Katya shrugged. "I thought it would be unhealthy for you to be aware of my emotional turmoil."

Kennedy gawped. "You had emotional turmoil?"

Nicole hid her smile by drinking more coffee.

Katya rolled her eyes. Obviously the coffee had helped her regain her composure. "Thank you for this most reviving drink, Nicole." She emitted the most elegant, subtle of sighs. "It will help. I promised Kennedy I'd help search for Maddox."

"I'll go." Nicole stood up. "You should stay with your daughter."

"But you're the nurse," Katya reasoned. "You should stay, in case something goes wrong."

"Nothing will go wrong," Nicole promised Katya. At the same time, a warmth flushed through her, not entirely caused by the Bailey's and coffee. Katya trusted her with her daughter and the new baby. Katya had stepped down from her pedestal. Perhaps they could never be friends, but possibly she and Kennedy's mother, Sebastian's former wife, could be allies.

Katya glanced toward the window, almost completely iced over by blowing snow. She shivered delicately. "Perhaps I will stay here . . . with my daughter."

Nicole didn't hesitate. "Of course," she agreed, heading to the hall and her coat.

35

❄

Snix snored so enormously he woke himself. It took him a moment to realize where he was—he'd slept in so many different places during his young life.

He was lying in straw inside a shed, warm as warm could be, cuddled next to his boy Maddox.

But Maddox was *crying*.

Snix sat up and licked Maddox's cheeks. The tears tasted salty and made Snix even hungrier.

"Oh, Pooh," Maddox sniffled. "I don't know what to do. I want my mommy and daddy. I want to go home."

Snix sat up straight, attempting to look large and confident. For one thing, he knew he had to think of himself as *Pooh* if he wanted to stay with the boy, and oh boy, did he want to stay with this boy. For another thing . . . well, what? What could he do?

He wagged his tail, hopefully. He gave a yip of encouragement. He tried to look bright-eyed.

His stomach growled.

Maddox's stomach growled.

Perhaps . . . Pooh chewed a stick of straw. Nope, didn't work. He spit it out.

Snow whirled into the shed, glittering in the glow from the spotlight.

"We've got to go back out there, Pooh." Maddox stood up. "We've got to go home."

Pooh yapped once.

Maddox frowned. He thought out loud: "I'm sure they'll take me back." Looking down at Pooh, he clenched his fists. "But I won't let them take you away from me, Pooh. I'll protect you. Even if we have to run away again."

Pooh's heart sank. He wasn't sure he could survive much longer without food.

"MADDOX? MADDOX!"

Running footsteps came toward them. Snow exploded as four booted feet stomped through the drifts in front of the shed. Two huge figures fell on their knees.

"Maddox." The boy's father reached out and clutched the boy to him. "Maddox, hey guy, I'm so glad I found you. What a smart kid you are to discover such a warm place to stay. Aren't you hungry? Don't you want to go home? Your mommy and grandmommy and Nicole are so worried about you. Granddad and I have been looking everywhere for you."

Pooh watched as the boy's father ran his hands over the boy's head and body, as if checking to be certain he was still all there.

"I'm sorry, Daddy, don't be mad at me—"

"I'm not mad, Maddox. Granddad and I are so glad to find you—"

"Maddox, you need a hat. Take mine." Granddad pulled his wool cap over the boy's head.

Pooh trembled as he heard the humans babble, everyone talking at once. The great big men had tears in their eyes. They hugged and touched Maddox as if he were the most precious thing in the world.

"Come on, Mad Man. We're going home. It's Christmas Eve." The daddy lifted Maddox up in his arms and held him tight.

Pooh whimpered, just a tiny whimper that kind of slipped out . . .

"I want Pooh!" Maddox wriggled in his father's arms. "I won't go without Pooh."

Pooh shivered with hope and terror.

Two huge arms reached in and picked Pooh up. "I've got Pooh," the grandfather said. "He's coming home with us, too."

"*In the house*," Maddox stipulated.

"Of course in the house," said the daddy. "We wouldn't leave a puppy out in the cold on a night like this."

The granddaddy wrapped the outside of his coat around Pooh. "We need to give this dog some food. I can feel his ribs."

The men set off tramping through the falling snow. They passed Sweet Inspirations with its windows full of candy. They passed Zero Main with its bright Christmas wreath. They passed Petticoat Row Bakery with its windows full of gingersnaps and cookies shaped like stars. They zigzagged around the tall brick Jared Coffin House, which had been standing since 1845 and still stood undaunted in the ferocious blizzard.

Pooh could feel the granddaddy's heart beating. The man's arms were big and held him much more securely than Maddox's thin arms had done—not that Pooh was complaining about Maddox, who was his true champion and best friend.

They went up Centre Street, past the Congregational Church. They forked left onto Westchester. Most of the houses were dark and closed, but one house glowed with light.

"Back door," the granddaddy yelled. "We're covered with snow. We can kick off our boots in the mudroom."

Pooh sagged. His memories of the mudroom were not good ones. The woman who didn't like dogs, the yelling . . .

He had no choice. He could struggle out and run away, but where would he go? Surely this time they would allow him to stay.

Doors opened and closed. Pooh was set on the floor. Boots were kicked off, scattering snow onto the already wet throw rug.

Pooh saw a pair of men's feet in red socks leave the room. Then a man's feet in brown socks left.

"We found him!" the daddy yelled.

"Oh, thank heavens!" Voices poured from the front of the house.

"Good Lord!" one of the men cried.

Shouts of jubilation rose and what sounded like dozens of voices intertwined. A thin baby's wail sirened through the noise and the voices softened.

Pooh sat in the mudroom, dripping, probably smelling of wet dog hair, *alone*.

"This calls for champagne," a man announced.

Footsteps grew closer to the kitchen. Pooh peered around the door. Only his nose and eyes . . .

"Hey, you." The granddaddy saw Pooh looking.

Pooh flinched and went small.

"We didn't forget you." The granddaddy lifted Pooh up, carried him a few feet, and set him down again. "But we've got a new baby in the house, the prettiest little girl you've ever seen. My goodness, there is no end to the wonders that can happen. Leave the house for thirty minutes and come home to a granddaughter!" He poured milk into a bowl and set the bowl in the microwave. The man opened the freezer and scrabbled around, all the while singing "Jingle Bells."

Pooh reflected silently, but not unhappily, that human beings were odd.

"Here," said the granddaddy. "I warmed the milk in the microwave. Drink up while I thaw some meatloaf for you, little fellow. Don't tell Nicole. She won't miss it anyway, with all the food in the house. Now where's the champagne?"

Pooh lapped up the warm milk as fast as his pink tongue could go while the man gathered glasses and popped a cork and set them on a tray.

"Dinner is served, your majesty." The man set a plate in front of Pooh. Suddenly, while Pooh watched, he pulled his sweater off over his head and piled it on the floor next to the vent. "Here. When you're through eating, you can rest on this. I'm too damned hot with all this excitement." He picked up the tray and started to leave the room. Stopping, he said to Pooh with a serious tone, "No accidents now, okay?"

Pooh sat down, lifted his head into its most noble pose

and remained still, doing the best he could to signal his comprehension and agreement.

The man chortled. "You're a smart one, aren't you?" He hurried away.

Pooh dove into the plate of warm delicious meatloaf.

36

❄

The living room was crowded with people all talking at once. Nicole took off the coat she'd just put on and settled into a chair in the corner to watch the grand reunion. Kennedy handed the baby to Katya and opened her arms to Maddox who threw himself into her embrace. James stood swaying in front of the baby, looking so green Nicole thought he might vomit.

James fell on his knees in front of his wife and took her face in his hands.

"How did you do this?" he asked, his face shining with tears. "We weren't gone more than half an hour, and you had the baby? Are you okay? Do you need to go to the hospital? It's a girl? How can it be a girl? Kennedy, I love you."

Katya sank gracefully into another armchair, both arms supporting her tiny granddaughter. "When I had Kennedy," she mused aloud, "I didn't *comprehend* her at first. I was sort of dozy on painkillers of some sort. Look at this splendid infant. She seems so peaceful."

Maddox squirmed away from his mother and ran to Katya. "Let me see her, Grandmama."

Katya held the bundle out for Maddox to see. "Careful," she warned. "The baby is brand-new and fragile."

As she viewed the lucky family—James with Kennedy, Katya with Maddox and the baby, Nicole allowed herself a moment of self-indulgence. She was spent. The adrenaline and calm ecstasy of practiced, knowledgeable, focused skill that had flooded her when Kennedy began to give birth drained away now, leaving her limp. She was not as young as she used to be. She'd done all the kneeling and bracing and assisting and cleaning with the swift ease of a ballerina, but right now her joints and muscles informed her they needed a nice hot bath with Epsom salts.

Her emotions were in upheaval, too. The birth of a baby was always—to use a terribly overused word—an *awesome* event. She hadn't recovered yet from the anxiety, like background music in her mind, that something was wrong with Kennedy or the baby, or could go wrong during the delivery, or, she hardly dared think it, that *she* could have done something wrong. If she hadn't been a trained nurse and a mature adult, she would have shrieked and screamed right along with Kennedy all through the delivery. The effort of pretending to be calm had taken its toil on her strength.

She could scarcely summon up the energy to keep the proper expression on her face, a smile that asserted "I'm so happy for you all," instead of a childish pout declaring "Doesn't anyone care about *me*?" and she felt wearily guilty about that.

Sebastian entered the living room with a tray of flutes and an opened bottle of champagne. He set it on the side table by the window. "Champagne for everyone."

"Even me?" Maddox asked.

Sebastian and the other adults laughed indulgently.

"It's a special day, so you may have a sip of mine," James told his son.

Sebastian couldn't stop smiling. He stepped away from the table for a moment, drawn inexorably to the sight of his granddaughter. He leaned over the back of the chair where Katya sat holding the baby while Maddox raised himself up on tiptoes to peek at the blanketed bundle.

There they were, Nicole thought. Everyone together who belongs together. By the window, the tall Christmas tree she'd decorated twinkled like love made visible. In the fireplace the logs burned low, crackling with sparks as the bark snapped. Stockings hung from the mantel. The crèche sat in perfection on the table. Nicole didn't belong in this intimate, elementary family group. She had learned in harder times how to steel her heart, and now she did her best to remember. She took deep breaths. She tried to count her blessings.

The phone rang.

"The phones are working again," Nicole noted to no one in particular.

Sebastian answered. His tense shoulders softened. "Katya? It's for you."

Katya hesitated, briefly, before laying the baby in James's arms. She reached for the phone.

"Hello?" Katya's voice was wary.

While the others watched, Katya's face began to glow. "Yes, I miss you, too. Wait a moment." Putting her hand over the receiver, she said, "It's Alonzo. I'll take this into the other room." She left, head high, triumphant.

Father Christmas, I owe you one, Nicole thought. Exchanging glances with Sebastian, she could see he was thinking the same thing.

Suddenly, Maddox flew across the room and pitched himself at Nicole. Hauling himself up onto her lap, the little boy leaned against her. "Nicole, Pooh is in the kitchen," he whispered.

Maddox's sweet breath in her ear, his easy confidence in her being his friend, expanded Nicole's heart into confetti and fireworks. For a moment, she couldn't speak.

She cleared her throat. "That's wonderful, Maddox. Is he okay?"

"Yes. I kept him warm all through the storm."

"Maybe he needs something to eat," Nicole suggested.

"Oh, yes!"

Sebastian was pouring the champagne and handing it around.

"I'll be right back for mine," Nicole told him.

Maddox took her hand and pulled her from the room, down the hall to the kitchen, where Pooh lay curled up on Sebastian's sweater, snoring, deeply asleep. An empty bowl and plate were on the floor.

"It looks like Granddad has already fed Pooh," Nicole said. Dropping down to Maddox's level, she put her hands on his shoulders. "You must be hungry, too, after your adventures. Can I fix you something?"

Maddox's eyes sparkled. "You make the best grilled cheeses, Nicole."

"Then I'll make you one right now," she said, and set to work, while Maddox sat next to Pooh, scratching him softly just behind the ears.

37

❄

Christmas Eve passed in a blur for Kennedy.

While her father drove off in the blizzard to fetch a friend of his who was a physician, James helped her into their bedroom so she could shower and slip on her maternity nightgown. Dr. Morris turned out to be an older woman, even calmer than Nicole, with gentle hands and a way of humming when she examined Kennedy. Not only did she pronounce Kennedy in A-plus condition, she presented her with a box of pads she'd brought from the hospital, a great relief for Kennedy on this night when every drugstore in town was shut tight. Overloaded with emotion and the drama of the evening, Kennedy thought that this humble, ordinary gift meant more than silver and gold.

Dr. Morris checked the baby, proclaiming her perfectly healthy. She put the necessary antibiotic ointment on her eyes, before, obviously pleased to be so useful, presenting Kennedy with a bag she'd prepared at the hospital. It held disposable diapers, tiny cotton shirts and several sleep rompers with infinitely small cotton cuffs that folded over the baby's hands to prevent her from scratching her face.

After Sebastian drove Dr. Morris home, Nicole set out a buffet on the dining room table: the beef Wellington sliced into pieces, vegetables, warm bread. No one sat at the table, but wandered here and there with a plate and a glass, perching on the edge of a chair, saying over and over again, "Isn't it amazing? Can you believe she's here? And on Christmas Eve!" Everyone was still animated and vaguely flustered, constantly peeking at the baby as if to be certain she really existed.

After some discussion, James helped Maddox rouse the sleepy little dog and take him out into the backyard where the animal performed his physical duties with alacrity, then raced back into the house. Tonight, James and Kennedy agreed, during a private conference, Pooh could sleep on the floor in Maddox's bedroom. After all, Kennedy thought with a private, slightly guilty smugness, if the dog did something on the rug, it wouldn't be her job to deal with it.

Because Pooh was allowed to sleep in his room, Maddox went to bed easily, and after his adventurous evening, he fell asleep at once. The dog, James told Kennedy, curled up on the rug next to the bed as if he considered himself Maddox's protector.

Kennedy was thankful that Maddox had the animal at least for a few nights. It would keep him from feeling excluded in the commotion over the new baby. Perhaps she'd even let him keep the dog.

Kennedy was utterly drained. Her head swam with the buzz of her family's conversation. People loomed up at her like boats through the fog.

"How is she?" Sebastian asked, or James, or Katya.

"Is she still sleeping?" Katya inquired, or Sebastian, or James.

"Would you like me to hold her while you eat?" offered James, or Katya, or Sebastian.

Nicole came to her rescue. "Kennedy, you shouldn't overexert yourself. It's time for you to get in bed and go to sleep."

"But the baby, where will she sleep?" Kennedy worried.

"In a dresser drawer, just as infants have throughout the centuries."

Kennedy recoiled with dismay. "The wood will be so hard."

Nicole shook her head. "I've lined it with quilts. Besides, she'll probably end up in bed with you and James."

Nicole showed Kennedy how to wrap the baby "like a

burrito"—so snugly the baby felt as contently secure as she had been Kennedy's belly.

"Now go to bed and get some sleep. We're not as wiped out as you are. In fact, we're all rather overexcited. So until we all go to bed," Nicole told Kennedy, "someone out here in the living room will hold your baby."

"I want to hold her," Kennedy confessed. "I don't want to let her go."

"The best thing you can do for her now," Nicole assured her, "is sleep."

"I'll see you in the morning, darling." Katya kissed Kennedy's forehead. "Before I leave for Boston."

Nothing had ever felt as soft as the plump mattress Kennedy lay on. Clouds, or perhaps it was a down comforter, warmed her weary body. Sleep came at once.

And good thing, for when the baby's thin cry from the drawer woke her at four in the morning, everyone else was asleep. Next to her on the bed, James snored loudly, a chainsaw noise that drowned out his daughter's cries.

Kennedy lifted her daughter from the dresser drawer and carried her into the living room. She changed her diaper and wrapped her snugly again. She decided to rest on the sofa, holding the infant in her arms.

The windows were black with deep night. The blizzard had passed. The wind was gone. It was silent throughout the house and over the island. The fire had burned out in the fireplace, but the room was still warm. Kennedy turned on the lights of the Christmas tree to keep her company as she rested with her babe in her arms.

She couldn't believe her good fortune. Now she had a son and a daughter, and a husband who loved them. Her mother was leaving in the morning to meet Alonzo in Boston. And now she could finally admit it: Kennedy had never seen her father look so happy as when he was with Nicole.

As for Nicole—all Kennedy's animosity had vanished, replaced by the cheering assurance that she would have her father's new, steady-handed and knowledgeable wife in her life as she went forward as a mother. She wished she had some way to thank Nicole, to express her inexpressible appreciation for all she'd done. What could she possibly do to articulate her gratitude?

In the morning, Kennedy decided sleepily, she'd tell James what she'd like to name their new daughter.

Nicole Katya Noel.

ABOUT THE AUTHOR

NANCY THAYER is the *New York Times* bestselling author of *Island Girls*, *Summer Breeze*, *Heat Wave*, *Beachcombers*, *Summer House*, *Moon Shell Beach*, and *The Hot Flash Club*. She lives in Nantucket.

ABOUT THE TYPE

This book was set in Goudy, a typeface designed by Frederick William Goudy (1865–1947). Goudy began his career as a bookkeeper, but devoted the rest of his life to the pusuit of "recognized quality" in a printing type. Goudy was produced in 1914 and was an instant bestseller for the foundry. It has generous curves and smooth, even color. It is regarded as one of Goudy's finest achievements.